"It's a bride's necklace.

"I might not make it to your wedding," Grandy said, "so I'd like to see Craig Smith put it on you."

Fortunately, Lyssa's grandmother thought he was a Smith, not a Rival, Craig thought as he unclasped the heirloom and placed it around Lyssa's neck.

"Craig," Grandy said, "You must kiss your bride."

Craig lowered his lips, but he was unprepared for the jolt of desire that rocketed the length of him as their mouths melded in a sensuous kiss— a kiss meant to be brief, a kiss that lasted too long.

"You'll be happy now, Lyssa," Grandy murmured.

Would she? Lyssa wondered. Or was Craig Rival involved in the recent attacks on her?

Dear Reader,

Be prepared to meet a "Woman of Mystery"!

This month, we're proud to bring you another story in our ongoing WOMEN OF MYSTERY program, designed to bring you the debut books of writers new to Harlequin Intrigue.

Meet Adrianne Lee, author of *Something Borrowed, Something Blue.*

Adrianne Lee is a native of Washington State. She is married to her high school sweetheart, has three grown daughters, two sons-in-law, two granddaughters and one grandson. Her hobbies include driving her 1937 Chevy sedan, "Bashful," to Hod Rod events in the Northwest. This is actually her third woman-in-jeopardy novel, but her very first for Harlequin Intrigue. Adrianne loves hearing from readers and encourages you to write to her at P.O. Box 158, Cle Elum, WA 98922.

We're dedicated to bringing you the best new authors, the freshest new voices. Be on the lookout for more upcoming titles in our "WOMEN OF MYSTERY" program!

Sincerely,

Debra Matteucci
Senior Editor and Editorial Coordinator
Harlequin Books
300 East 42nd Street, Sixth Floor
New York, NY 10017

Something Borrowed, Something Blue

Adrianne Lee

Harlequin Books

TORONTO • NEW YORK • LONDON
AMSTERDAM • PARIS • SYDNEY • HAMBURG
STOCKHOLM • ATHENS • TOKYO • MILAN
MADRID • WARSAW • BUDAPEST • AUCKLAND

For Pete and Carl Pozzi, my wonderful parents, who gave me the two greatest gifts in life: roots and wings.

Special thanks to Ruth Craven, Ed D, RN and Sheila Keener, BSN, RN of the U.W. School of Nursing, and Rich Marlow of Marlow's Fine Jewelry.

ISBN 0-373-22296-3

SOMETHING BORROWED, SOMETHING BLUE

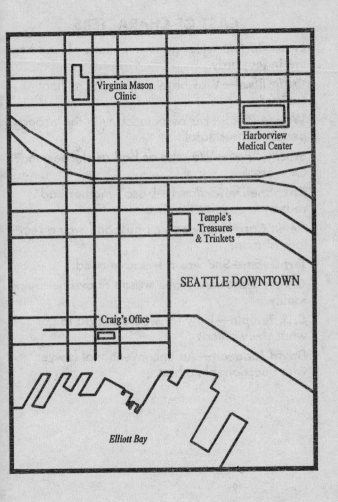

CAST OF CHARACTERS

Lyssa Carlyle—Her good intentions placed her life in jeopardy.

Craig Rival—Was he Lyssa's savior or her stalker?

Wayne Rival—His association with the wrong people proved fatal.

Stacey Rival—Was she as bad as she seemed? Or worse?

Roxanne DeHaviland—Lyssa's mother had reason to despise the Rivals.

Kevin Carlyle—Lyssa's ex-husband was a real ladies' man.

Teri Dean—She was a friend in need.

Ginger Van Allen—She wasn't above betraying family.

C. J. Temple—How far would she go to get what she wanted?

David Lundeen—An unconventional lawyer with questionable ethics.

Prologue

Monday

"Wayne Rival won't be causing any more problems." The speaker braced the telephone receiver between chin and shoulder and glanced at the middle-aged man sprawled on the floor. The glassy hazel eyes seemed to stare back. Nudging the dead man's ribs with the toe of one boot, the person grinned. *Who'd have guessed killing could be such a rush. The blood in my veins feels electrified.*

Listening to the voice at the other end of the line, the speaker sighed impatiently. "Yes, yes, yes. I've got it right here." Greedy eyes gazed down at the necklace draped across one gloved hand. The DeHaviland Purity. The wedding necklace. A heavy handful of pure blue-white, pear-cut diamonds, half carats each, except for the two-carat centerpiece, were set in swirls of solid gold, its blue brilliance nearly blinding. "This piece of the 1800s is our ticket to easy street."

Listening again, the killer recalled the one thing that hadn't come off quite right. "Don't worry about that. I know what to do next. But there is a problem—*she* saw me."

Another pause.

"I don't care if Rival's bad heart *was* common knowledge! What if someone discovers the truth? She can put me here at the right time."

The speaker listened again, and felt the earlier exhilaration eroding to anger. "That's easy for you to say. I'm the one taking the risks. Okay, okay. We'll talk about it later. I have to get out of here before the tide comes in."

Hanging up, the person jammed the Purity into a waist pouch, next to the faux, an excellent copy of the necklace, and an empty vial, and zipped it shut. Quickly, the person scrubbed out the two drink glasses on the table, dried them and put them in the cupboard, took a fresh glass from the shelf, pressed Wayne's fingers around it, then poured whiskey and cola into it and tipped it over near the edge of the counter. The amber liquid spread rapidly, pooled in the tiled grooves and dribbled onto the floor.

Satisfied, the person reached for the phone again and dialed 911.

"Emergency Services," a voice answered.

"Help me...." The words were spoken in a muffled, genderless moan. "My heart...the pain." The speaker let the receiver slip loose and hit the hardwood floor with a loud *clunk,* then tiptoed around Wayne Rival's lifeless form, exited silently through the back door and fled across the deck.

Within minutes, the person was on the beach, hastening through the moonless night on damp sand, headed for the spot where a dark Cadillac awaited. Hot breath fogged in the cold air. The going was awkward. Worrying thoughts plagued. If it hadn't been for *her,* tonight would have gone as smooth as child's play.

Anger throbbed at the killer's temples during the scramble up the embankment and out onto the North Shore Road. Luckily, the road was deserted, but in the distance a siren wailed. Likely the first-aid car. *Have to hurry.*

Panting, the killer dropped behind the wheel, started the car and fishtailed onto the road. Halfway to Belmont State Park, the first-aid car came barreling past. The killer edged the Cadillac to the shoulder, slowing momentarily, then continued on.

The adrenaline rush was leveling off. Heartbeat was steadying. It had gone perfectly. Well, almost perfectly. *Contrary to what my partner thinks, the woman is a loose end I can't afford to leave untied. Lyssa Carlyle is living on borrowed time.*

Chapter One

Three nights later

She wasn't actually committing a crime, only recovering what belonged to her. She'd just slip into Windance, find the faux Purity and head back to Arizona on the next flight.

Of course, if she were caught in the act...

Well, Lyssa Carlyle determined, she'd make certain that didn't happen. She wasn't leaving Washington State without the necklace. Not this time. She should have known better than to trust a Rival. No matter how kind Wayne had seemed, he'd proven her family's disdain for his family was valid. His sudden death was a shock, but it would take more than that to stop her.

Still, the deed couldn't be accomplished soon enough. She pressed the gas pedal of her rented Mazda RX7 to the floor, thinking of her grandmother and how much what she was about to do would mean to the dying woman. A twinge of guilt nudged her conscience, but she refused to give it heed. The deception was necessary.

As she passed the entrance to Belmont State Park, on the north shore of Hood Canal, headlights in her rearview mirror caught her eye. Lyssa frowned.

A car was speeding toward her. She tapped the brake, edging toward the shoulder. The huge, dark-colored Cadillac moved into the lane beside her. Lyssa saw nothing through its opaque windows. It swerved closer. She stiffened, alarmed. The big automobile grazed her door. A metallic screech rang out.

Cursing, she stomped on the brake. The Mazda stopped. The Cadillac spurted past. Lyssa swore again, but the squeal of tires biting pavement cut off her diatribe. Unbelievably, the Cadillac was backing toward her. "What the—?"

Before she could react, it smashed her door a second time, harder than the first. The blow jolted her and the car sideways, closer to the ditch.

Tears of terror sprang to her eyes. *Move, Lyssa! Move!* There was no telling what kind of psycho was driving that tank, or what his intentions were if he got his hands on her. Unwilling to find out, Lyssa yanked the steering wheel to the left and slammed her foot on the gas pedal. Tires whined and spat rocks as the Mazda shot ahead of its pursuer. Her heart slapped against her rib cage. Wind funneled through her open window, pulling pins from her coiled hair.

How was she going to escape? This road was only twenty-five miles long—and as twisted as the maniac chasing her. Lighted areas were few and far between, driving more treacherous with each bend. Her palms were clammy. She gripped the steering wheel tighter.

Around the next curve, Lyssa crossed the center line. Headlights came at her. A scream tore from her throat. She cranked the wheel to the right, barely missing the oncoming vehicle. Its horn's angry blast echoed a reprimand as her car bounced back from the bumpy shoulder.

Lyssa began to tremble. *Stifle this fear! Think!* She forced herself to count to ten, then drew a wobbly breath. Her only hope was to lengthen the distance between the two cars, pull into a side road and hide. She downshifted, jammed the gas pedal and gained speed across a lonely stretch that veered away from the canal for a mile or two, toward a tiny inlet where the Tahuya River emptied into the larger body of water. The road narrowed over a small bridge, then widened on the other side, swinging in a ninety-degree angle back to the main waterway.

She took the small bridge too fast. Rubber yelped. The Mazda skidded along the pavement. Its headlight beams bobbed across the dark terrain.

Lyssa eased off the gas until she had the car under control. Then, with her chest threatening to explode, she jammed the pedal to the floor. Wind gushed through the open window, took the last of her hairpins and freed her long tresses. She tugged hair from her face and checked the rearview mirror. Although she was outrunning the Cadillac, its headlights were still visible.

Wasn't there a side street just ahead? She scoured the landscape, cursing. "Where is that road?"

She rounded the next bend. A large, dark shape suddenly appeared in her lane. *A frightened deer!*

Lyssa screamed. She jerked the steering wheel to the right.

Missing the deer by inches, she drove onto the shoulder. The Mazda bounced out of control. A huge boulder loomed in her path. Her arms flew to her face and "CRASH" reverberated through her mind. Both feet hit the brake. The engine stalled. The car bucked. Slowed. Skidded. The front end crunched into the rock.

Lyssa jerked forward. Her seat belt cut into her chest, but the restraint kept her forehead from hitting the windshield by a fraction of an inch. Flopping back against the seat, she sat in stunned silence. The deer had vanished.

Headlights glared across the sky from behind, growing ever brighter. Lyssa flipped off the seat belt, grasped the door handle and pushed. It was jammed. The sound of the approaching car grew louder. Hooking the shoulder strap of her purse over her neck, she scrambled out the passenger door.

About ten feet ahead of her car was a stand of trees. She darted into them and slumped against a stout pine, breathing tiny, rapid gulps of pungent night air.

The Cadillac squealed around the corner. Its lights caught her car. The smell of burning rubber bit at Lyssa's nostrils as the huge car skidded to a stop. The driver's door popped open. She rammed her back against the rough bark of the tree and, holding her breath, strained to hear above her thundering heart.

A full ten seconds passed. Warily, she peered around the tree. A raincoat-clad figure was standing at the open door of the Mazda, peering inside. A hat was pulled low, hiding the person's face. She couldn't tell if it was a man or a woman. The person straightened and raised both arms over the roof of Lyssa's car.

The Cadillac's headlights clearly outlined an imposing metal bar held in the person's gloved hands. As the
arms descended, Lyssa barely stopped herself from
shouting a protest.

A clang rang through the night air.

She winced, feeling the blow as surely as if it had
struck her. *She couldn't stay here.*

Across the street, less than fifteen feet away, she
discerned the slap of water hitting shore. She shot a
leery glance at the Cadillac. Now was the time to make
her move. She could cross the street unseen, unless the
person rummaging through the Mazda was not alone.
That fear momentarily held her in place. But if she
stayed where she was, she would surely be caught.

The person on the road returned to the Cadillac and
started rifling in the glove box. Trembling all over,
Lyssa zipped across the street. She reached the other
side just as a powerful flashlight beam landed on the
spot she had occupied seconds before. A low whistle
of relief pushed through her lips. She half slid, half fell
down the six-foot bank to the beach, grateful for the
noise-concealing slurps of the tidewater.

Lyssa raced across the wet sand. Broken shells
crunched beneath her feet. Water licked hungrily at
the soles of her high-top sneakers. Was the tide coming in or going out? The moonless dark offered no
clue. How had she ended up in this sick scenario, with
fate intent on keeping her from getting what was
rightfully hers?

Lyssa glanced over her shoulder to see if she was
being followed. She saw nothing, heard no one. Her
anxious fingers tugged the leather strap of her purse
and checked the zipper. Thank God. She hadn't lost

the back-door key to Windance that Wayne had given her. But . . . a worrisome thought nagged at her. Had she left anything in her carry-on bag that would lead her pursuer to Wayne Rival's house? Try as she might, she couldn't remember.

Biting down panic, Lyssa attempted to estimate her distance from Windance. The Tahuya river was behind her, and although the darkness obscured familiar landmarks, a few property owners were in residence; irregular lights dotted the shoreline, offering a sporadic road map of sorts. She figured she should have less than a mile to go.

Her strides increased. Endless surges of freezing water rushed at her until goose bumps rippled her flesh. The salty, dead-fish stench punctuated every breath she drew. She forced herself to think of the hot shower and the warm, dry clothing only minutes away, and felt encouraged.

But the water edged higher on her shoes.

With heart-wrenching dread, Lyssa realized the tide was coming in. She tried running faster. Waves broke around her calves, sucking at her footing, impeding her efforts. Cold stung her legs through her saturated jeans. Again the water attacked. Slimy tendrils of seaweed wrapped around her ankles, tripping her. She pitched to the wet sand. Sharp shell fragments bit into her flesh, shooting pain through her palms and knees. Hot tears filled her eyes, but she refused to let them overcome her.

She struggled to a kneeling position. The surf charged, bumping her into a cement seawall. Spitting bitter salt water, Lyssa staggered to her feet and stumbled forward. Fear trudged with her as the water stormed again and again. Then it dawned on her that there were only two cement seawalls in this area. Wayne's and the one she had just passed. It belonged to the Burleys, Wayne's nearest neighbors. The thought of seeking their help slowed her pace. But the Burley place was dark.

She moved toward the bank. From here to a hundred feet before Windance, the shoreline abutted the road. Headlights poked the darkness above her head. She glimpsed a large, dark car. Lyssa ducked, squatting in the icy water, listening to the automobile rumble down the road.

Trapped air burst from her lungs. Lurching to her feet, she hurried ahead. Tens seconds later, she spotted her destination. Exhausted, Lyssa half swam, half waded through the thigh-high waves, stumbled up the seawall steps and collapsed in a heap on Wayne's deck.

She was safe.

CRAIG RIVAL SWORE in frustration. Four times he'd punched in the code and four times the wrought-iron gate had refused to budge. The glowing red light on the computerized security box assured him the system was working. In spite of this, he gripped the metal fence on either side of the opening and shook the gate. "Damn!"

Someone had obviously changed the security code. He'd have to open the gate from inside the house, if he could find a way to get in. The tide wouldn't go out enough to allow him to enter from the beach side for hours, and he couldn't remember having a worse case of jet lag.

Behind him, his rented Cadillac purred. Ignoring it, Craig craned his neck and peered between the weathered bars, past the tree-lined drive, to the sprawling residence in the distance. He shook his head in wonder. It wasn't new to him, but it was still impressive.

Windance. A woebegone smile crossed his lips. His father had named the huge L-shaped house for the way the wind made whitecaps dance across the water. The grounds stretched four hundred feet across and were surrounded by water on three sides. A breezeway separated the main structure from a five-car garage to his left, and a deck angled over the canal to his right. Pole lights dotted the grounds, spilling eerie yellow pools across the building and drive.

On a bright sunny day there was no place more inviting, but right now, shadowed by the dark sky, with the smell of rain in the air, it struck Craig as a gloomy reminder of all that he'd lost and could never recover. He returned to the rented car, shut off the motor, tossed his suitcoat across the front seat, then pressed the trunk-release button.

After his father's tragic death last September, he couldn't bear to set foot inside Windance. He'd closed the house, left the running of Rival Gems International to his uncle Wayne, the company's manager, and headed to Europe. He lifted the trunk lid and shoved his suitcase to one side.

The yearlong trip hadn't entirely been an exercise in escapism. He'd picked up and sent back a few good pieces of estate jewelry, in particular, the Russian czarina's tiara, which he'd instructed Wayne to make the centerpiece of "the Collection."

Hefting a tire iron, he slammed the trunk, returned to the fence and began systematically checking the weathered bars for weak spots. But his thoughts were on the Collection. From the time he was a young boy, Craig had questioned his father's refusal to sell certain items of jewelry at any price. Paul Rival would gaze down at the specially designed display case, skim his hand across the smooth glass cover as though he were caressing a sleek cat and smile that secret smile. "Some things, my son, no amount of money can replace." His reasoning eluded Craig.

Then Paul had died, and Craig understood the meaning of his father's words all too well. The band around his heart tightened. What cruel irony that Wayne, too, should die at Windance, and at the very time Craig had decided to come home. But why Wayne had been here remained a mystery.

The chilly September night air penetrated his thin shirt, dispersing his weighty thoughts. At last he found two of the iron fence posts near the right edge of the fence that felt weak enough to be forced out.

The headlights of a vehicle approaching Bald Point, near the road's end, fanned the grounds, the house, the deck, momentarily stilled, continued to draw near, then were snuffed.

Teenagers parking, Craig supposed, applying the tire iron to the fence and levering his weight against the tool. The tinny clash stabbed the quietude.

Wincing at the bleating alarm he'd triggered, Craig wrenched the two rusty posts apart, then squeezed his lean frame through and headed up the drive. The damp air drew goose bumps across his flesh. About ten feet from the house, he halted, staring at the red shutters sandwiching each window. Absently, he tapped his thigh with the tire iron.

The last thing he'd done before leaving here last September was secure the shutters. Now they stood open. Since receiving word of Wayne's fatal heart attack, he had pondered his uncle's presence at Windance, coming up with a couple of plausible reasons, but it looked as though Wayne had been using the house after Craig had asked him not to, Craig concluded. He felt annoyed and, as quickly, guilty for feeling annoyance toward a man who could not defend his actions.

Heavyhearted, he unlocked the door and strode into the spacious entry. A braided rug covered most of the foyer. With the thick cushion swallowing his footsteps, Craig padded to the opposite wall, groped for and found the switch.

Light transformed dark shapes into well-known objects. With a raised brow, Craig regarded the familiar trestle table and its companion antique bench. Both oak surfaces were exposed, the sheets he'd used to cover them flipped to the floor in crumpled heaps. Missing was the Dresden vase that belonged— A movement at the corner of his vision brought him spinning on his heel just in time to see the vase in question arcing toward his head.

He raised his arms too late. The vase struck his forehead and shattered. He dropped to his knees, the tire iron slipping from his slack hand. As blackness overtook him, Craig had the strangest impression that he'd been felled by a soaking wet, blond sea monster.

HER HEART TRIP-HAMMERING, Lyssa leaned over the unconscious man. Seawater and grit dripped from her hair and clothes onto his white shirt, his gray slacks and his handsome face. Her gaze bounced from the metal bar to the prone figure, and she felt a dizzying wave of relief. She'd avoided having her head bashed in by mere seconds.

Being caught in Windance was the least of her problems now. Lyssa hastened to the phone, dialed 911, quickly related the situation and got immediate assurance a police officer was on the way.

Back in the foyer, she deactivated the fence alarm. The jarring bleats stopped. Her nervous gaze swung to the man on the floor. He hadn't moved, but what if he came to before the police arrived? The disturbing possibility sent her digging through kitchen cupboards until she located a length of cheesecloth and some scissors.

"When I get through with you, buddy, you aren't going to be hurting anyone else," she promised, coiling a length of cheesecloth around his wrists. Using macramé skills she hadn't employed since her teen years, Lyssa trussed his hands behind his back, then stretched the makeshift rope to his ankles and cinched them together until his limbs and body formed a crooked O. She tested the knots. They'd probably hold.... She glanced toward the kitchen, deciding the phone was too far away.

Slipping and sloshing and depositing gritty smears in her wake, Lyssa dragged him on the cotton throw rug into the kitchen. Only then did she let herself relax enough to feel the cold of her saturated clothing and to wonder why this man had come after her. The face was not familiar. She didn't know him, had never seen him before that she could recall. Sighing, she concluded he was probably just a maniac and she'd never know his reasons. In fact, he likely didn't know the reasons himself.

A woman alone wasn't safe anywhere nowadays. Then again, perhaps she'd been so worried about Grandy and the necklace, she hadn't been as cautious as she usually was. A fat lot of good it did to realize that now. Her return to Arizona would be delayed precious hours, hours Grandy might not have.

Grandy was so certain her miracle was going to happen, so certain the wedding necklace would be returned to the family before she drew her last breath. Somehow Lyssa had to find the faux Purity and bring it to her in time. But time was running out. Thanks to this jerk. She felt like striking out at the unconscious man, but knew it would improve nothing, especially not her mood.

A sudden weariness settled over her. She ached to get out of the wet clothes and into a hot shower, but the thought of leaving the man unguarded, even to fetch a towel, started her trembling worse than ever. Lyssa retrieved the tire iron from the foyer. It felt as heavy as a bar of gold. Scooting her sodden bottom onto the tiled kitchen counter, she balanced the weapon across her thighs.

The only sounds in the house were the *plonk* of water dripping from her pant hem, puddling on the oak floor, and the man's steady breathing. At least, murder wouldn't be added to her Thursday night's activities, she thought. Her gaze steadied on her prisoner, tracing his features, his build, memorizing every detail. There would be no question of identification when she testified against him.

She had a talent for sizing people up at a glance. But this was different. It was hard to judge his height with him all scrunched up. Let's see, she had aimed the vase about five inches above her head, and she was five foot five.... Height: average. His shoulders were broad, his hips narrow.... Weight: average. His face—now that, at least, was not average. His nose and chin, even his lips, had a boldness she deemed downright sensuous. A wicked-looking lump, the size of a halved tennis ball, adorned the upper left corner of his forehead. It was scarlet against his disheveled blue-black hair. Lyssa shivered, feeling hot yet cold.

What had life done to this handsome man to turn him into a psychopath?

He groaned, and his black eyebrows twitched.

Lyssa flinched, and clutched the tire iron over her racing heart.

OUTSIDE, THE KILLER clutched the crowbar between frustrated fists and drew a ragged breath. *Damn! Waiting three days for the right moment, and when it comes, she escapes. Look at her, sitting on the counter. So close. So far away.*

A vision of cracking Lyssa across the skull with the heavy metal filled the watcher's mind, then dissolved in an angry exhalation of breath. If only she'd been caught on the road. Silencing her in this house was not appealing. The police weren't keen on coincidences. Another body at Windance might start them asking questions. Unwanted questions.

A police siren sounded far in the distance and sent an alarm straight through the watcher.

Lyssa Carlyle would be dealt with later.

When she was alone.

Sooner than she expected.

The killer hurried down the drive and squeezed through the new gap between the wrought-iron bars. Glancing from the old Caddy to the newer one parked next to the fence sparked an idea. "Seems I need some new wheels."

The killer hastened to the late-model Cadillac. It would be close—hot-wiring the Caddy, a skill learned years ago from necessity, and taking off before the police arrived—but not impossible. The killer doubted the siren could be heard inside the house yet.

Opening the driver's door flooded the inside of the newer car with light. Sliding onto the rich leather upholstery the killer moved aside a discarded gray suit jacket and stretched across the bench seat to reach the wiring under the dashboard. A jingle from the steering column caught the killer's attention. And evoked a smile. Protruding from the ignition were the car keys.

"Well, well, well. How very obliging."

Sitting up, the killer gripped the keys. The engine hummed to life. A moment later, the new Cadillac pulled onto the road, heading back to Belmont.

The police officer didn't even glance at it as the two cars passed on the Tahuya bridge.

Chapter Two

Where were the police? Lyssa peeled back the soggy cuff of her sweater and stared at her watch which, through some miracle of modern technology, was ticking away as efficiently as though it had not been doused in the canal. The sudden switch of digital numbers prompted a weary sigh. She had no idea how long ago she'd dialed 911—time hadn't been a priority at that moment, but it was getting to be. Her skin ached with cold and goose flesh. She sneezed.

Craig Rival groaned. His eyelids flashed open. The spinning room brought them slamming shut again. Pain throbbed inside his head, and he recalled too vividly being struck with the Dresden vase. Concussion? That would account for the delusions. He could have sworn he'd seen the sea monster again—sitting on the counter. Heaven knew he could smell it.

Lyssa thought she heard a movement on the porch outside the window. Startled, she spun toward the window. Was that someone moving through the darkness, or her own terror playing tricks on her? A moan from her prisoner chased the thought away and set her pulse leaping. Her racing blood vanquished some of her chill. She hopped to the floor.

The motion jostled Craig's body. His eyes blinked open. Less than four inches from his nose, two grimy tennis shoes stared back at him. He tried to sit up, but his limbs didn't respond. Had the blow to his skull left him paralyzed? He shook his head, hoping to clear the fog, but managed only to rouse a bevy of dancing stars.

Something prickled his cheek as the left side of his face reclaimed the cotton rug. Whiskers, he thought, closing his eyes. Need a shave. His spinning head throbbed. It occurred to him there was a flaw in his paralysis theory, but he hurt too much everywhere to reason it out. If only that awful odor would go away, he could think straighter.

The *swick* of wet denim brought Craig's eyes open a slit. A woman leaned over him, wielding the tire iron inches from his forehead. She wasn't a sea monster, although she certainly did smell and look like something fresh from the briny deep. Dark streaks underscored both of her cold sea green eyes, and seaweed and sand studded her face, her stringy hair and dank clothes. "Who the hell are you?"

"As if you don't know!" Lyssa shook her head. How dare this low-life piece of slime pretend he hadn't gone through her carry-on bag, the glove box of her car, seen the car-rental agreement?

Craig tried to straighten his limbs and realized with a jolt that his arms and legs were tied behind him. He gave a reflexive, ineffectual jerk on the bindings. "What the hell—? Lady, are you crazy or something?"

"How dare *you* call *me* crazy?" Was that a car motor she heard? She peered toward the window again, but could see nothing but her own reflection. She spun back to her prisoner.

The fanatical gleam in her eyes chilled Craig. She looked insane enough to crush his skull with that tire iron. He'd better try to humor her...until he thought of some way to get free. "Wh-what's going on?"

Lyssa shook her head. "Don't tell me cracking a vase on that thick skull of yours made you forget the past couple of hours?"

"Look, if it's money you want...I haven't much on me, but I can lay my hands on, uh—" How much would it take to get rid of her? "—uh, several thousand dollars...as soon as the banks open tomorrow."

Lyssa gave a derisive laugh. "I don't want your money."

Confusion arrowed through him. He struggled against his ties. "Then what do you want?"

Was that a siren she heard at last? Yes. Soon. The police would be here soon. A modicum of relief swept through her. "What I want is to know why you've been trying to kill me."

Wide-eyed with disbelief, Craig glared at the woman. "Why *I've* been trying to kill *you?* Lady, take a good look around, I'm the one who's been attacked in my own house and hog-tied like a roped calf at a rodeo."

Lyssa rolled her eyes toward the ceiling and laughed. "Your house?" The siren was closer, louder. Didn't he hear it?

"Yes, *my* house. I'm Craig Rival."

The name momentarily threw Lyssa. She didn't believe for one minute he was Wayne's nephew and heir, not with that blue-black hair, those coffee brown eyes. But he hadn't pulled Craig Rival's name from thin air. The creep was obviously a local. Lyssa clicked her tongue at the man. "You're a smooth one, I'll give you that. But for your information, Craig Rival won't even be back in this country until tomorrow."

How did she know that? "I took an earlier flight."

"Of c-course." Lyssa buried her nose against the grungy sweater plastered to her upper arm and sneezed. She could definitely hear a siren now.

Craig gave another frustrated yank on his tethers. "Dammit! I *am* Craig Rival!"

"And I'm Madonna!" Lyssa's teeth began to chatter.

"You should get out of those wet clothes."

Lyssa sucked in a sharp breath, then glowered at the man through narrowed eyelids and smacked her palm with the tire iron.

Craig tried to shrink away from her, his nose wrinkled in disgust. "Believe me, lady, the last thing I want is to see you naked, but your lips are blue and you're shaking like a bowl of gelatin. You're going to catch pneumonia."

"Spare me the concern. I wouldn't be s-s-sopping wet if it weren't for you." Lyssa sneezed again.

"Me? I don't know what you're taking about."

"Yeah, right." From outside, Lyssa caught the distinct wail of a siren gearing down and, for the first time in hours, she breathed easier.

"Look, Miss... uh...?" When it was obvious she wasn't going to fill in the blank, he continued. "My name is Craig Rival, and this is my kitchen floor you're dripping on."

"Mister, y-you're a b-broken record." She hugged herself against another onslaught of shivering.

"I can prove it. My ID is in my wallet."

"Yeah, and your wallet's where—in your other pants? I've already searched the ones you're wearing, and guess what? No wallet."

"I don't always carry my wallet in my pants."

"Then where is it?"

"In my suit jacket," Craig snapped at her in frustration.

His look of indignation ticked her. The man was incredible. "In case you haven't noticed, you're not wearing a jacket."

"Correct," Craig said, groaning. "I didn't want to ruin it on the fence. It's in my car. Outside the gate. Look, it'd only take a couple of minutes to check."

The sound of footsteps on the porch gave Lyssa heart. She leaned closer. "Tell the police. Maybe they'll buy your story."

"The police?" Had she actually been fool enough to call them? A sliver of hope knifed through Craig. He knew all the local cops by name. In a few minutes this mess would be cleared up and she'd be the one getting her fragrant hide hauled to jail.

A series of insistent buzzes jerked Lyssa's head toward the foyer. Rising, she gave Craig a derisive smile. "Ah—the cavalry sounds impatient. Maybe they'll just save the taxpayers' money and execute you now. By firing squad."

Lyssa left the room at a run.

Craig watched the departing woman's backside. She was a bit thin for his taste, but her wet clothes cleaved her curves in ways that under normal circumstances would tweak his imagination. However, there was nothing normal about his situation or this female. His pounding head wrenched a moan from him. *What a homecoming.* Realizing his hands and feet felt numb, Craig attempted to shift positions. Nothing helped. The cops hadn't arrived any too soon.

LYSSA HAD EXPECTED her rescuers to be the macho cops she watched on television shows. Instead, neither of the two uniformed police officers spotlighted beneath the porch light looked old enough to be out of high school.

The female officer referred to a palm-size tablet, then glanced down at Lyssa with questioning hazel eyes. "Ms. Carlyle?"

Lyssa nodded, then let loose with a hearty sneeze.

"I'm Officer Kaslow." Light brown hair hung down her back in a thick, no-nonsense braid, and her serious tone denied any inexperience Lyssa had been laying at her door. "This is my partner, Officer Dunn."

Officer Dunn had the pink-cheeked, milk white complexion of a little boy. His blond hair brushed the tips of his ears and the brim of his cap shadowed soft blue eyes. He held his lanky frame in a self-conscious slump.

Lyssa ushered them in and closed the door against the chilled night air. "Thank God, you're here. I don't th-think I could have held up m-much longer."

"Our report says you have the suspect tied up. Where is he?" the policeman asked.

"In th-there." Lyssa pointed.

Officer Dunn left the two women alone in the foyer and hurried into the kitchen. Lyssa rapidly related the sequence of events for Officer Kaslow up to and including her conversation with her prisoner.

"Are you a relative of the Rivals, Ms. Carlyle?" Officer Kaslow asked.

Lyssa hugged herself against another attack of shivers, but she was prepared for this question. She'd decided to tell the police the truth, just not all of it. "N-no. A business associate and friend."

"Then you know Craig Rival?"

"No. He's been in Europe since before his uncle and I met. In fact, I was here last weekend when he called from overseas. He's d-due home this Friday. Tomorrow."

TO CRAIG, IT SEEMED LIKE an aeon before he finally heard footsteps headed his way. He watched the doorway expectantly, rolling to his stomach and speaking over his shoulder the second he thought he recognized a familiar face. "Okay, Archer. The joke's gone on long enough. Hurry. Untie me before my hands and feet turn black. I want that crazy woman arrested."

The cop bent over Craig and tested the knots. "You aren't going anywhere just yet, mister."

Shock ricocheted from Craig's startled ears to his numb toes. This wasn't Bob Archer's voice. He struggled to his side and peered into the face of a stranger— young, new and probably a rookie. Craig had been gone a year. How could he have expected nothing would change? "Whatever that woman has told you is a lie. She broke into my house and attacked me with a vase when I came through the front door.''

The policeman rose and turned away. ''I have to check something outside. I'll be right back.''

''Don't leave me like this,'' Craig yelled at the departing cop. The effort sent shards of light skipping through his eyes. Dejectedly, he rested his aching head on the rug.

Within ten minutes, the rookie was back in the kitchen, standing over Craig. This time he introduced himself, then read Craig his rights.

''Do you understand these rights?'' Officer Dunn asked.

Craig strained off the carpet and cocked an eye toward the policeman. ''Yes, but all this can be cleared up if you'll just check in the Cadillac outside the fence for my ID.''

The policeman was scribbling on a tablet. He looked at Craig. ''I've already examined the car.''

Craig slumped to the floor in relief. ''So you know the truth. Then untie me.''

Ten seconds passed before he realized the policeman hadn't made a move toward him. His usually quick mind was slow in piecing together the most logical reason. He wrenched his neck an inch above the rug. ''You didn't find my ID, did you?'' The look on Officer Dunn's cherubic face was all the answer Craig needed. His voice roughened with desperation. ''Don't you see? That crazy woman must have stolen my wallet while I was unconscious. Call Bob Archer. He'll vouch for me.''

''Sergeant Archer is away on a fishing trip this week.''

"Then get someone else."

"Who?"

The policeman waited for an answer, but Craig couldn't get his fuzzy mind to release any other names. He shook his head and let loose a woebegone sigh.

"Mister, so far everything that woman says about you has checked out."

"Everything she— You actually believe I've been trying to kill her?"

"She claims you tried to run her car off the road with your car."

"She's lying!"

"Well, your Caddy says otherwise."

"What?" Craig frowned, then winced as a sharp pain stabbed his forehead.

"The damage to the passenger side of your vehicle substantiates her charges."

"Damage?" It was a nightmare. He'd wake soon and all would be normal.

The policeman's blue eyes narrowed. "Look, if this is your house, why did you break the fence to get in?"

"Someone changed the security combination." Craig's blood pressure rose to the beat of his temper, singeing his cheeks.

"Calm down." Officer Dunn firmly but gently pressed the palm of his hand against Craig's shoulder. "That's a nasty-looking bump on your head. I don't like the way your pupils are dilated. Unless I miss my guess, you've got a concussion."

So, he wasn't the only one who suspected a concussion. Being right gave Craig no satisfaction. The dismal prospect of being taken first to the hospital, then to the police station, before this mess could be straightened out loomed over him like a leaden blanket. Weariness seeped into his every pore, and he sagged against the rug. It was a relief to shut his heavy eyelids. "I'm lucky she didn't kill me. Probably going to lose my fingers and toes, though.... Can't feel them any longer...."

"Hey, Kaslow! Come in here. Call an ambulance while I untie this guy. His hands are turning blue and he seems to be drifting in and out of consciousness. I think it's a concussion."

Craig knew he wasn't unconscious. He'd heard the *thunk* of footsteps into the room, heard an unfamiliar female voice conversing with Dunn, and could now feel someone jerking on the ties at his hands and feet. He just couldn't open his eyes—no matter how hard he tried—but there was nothing wrong with his sense of smell. His nose wrinkled involuntarily. The fishy odor was back, stronger than ever.

Lyssa stood to one side, hugging herself as Officer Kaslow made the call and Officer Dunn cut the bindings from the other man's wrists and ankles.

To Craig, the voices over his head sounded far away, as though he was hearing them through a furnace vent.

Kaslow set the receiver aside and turned to Lyssa. "As a matter of record, I'll need to see some identification, Ms. Carlyle."

Carlyle? The name crabbed along the shorelines of Craig's muddled mind, trying to find a home, but he couldn't place it.

Lyssa retrieved her purse from the counter, dug out a waterlogged leather wallet and removed her wet driver's license. "Here. S-sorry about the c-condition.

My purse took a swim in the Canal w-with me." Her teeth were chattering worse than ever.

Kaslow studied the picture against the woman standing before her. "You're from Mesa, Arizona?"

"Yes."

"And your business is related to Rival Gems in Seattle?"

Lyssa nodded. "I design jewelry. Here's one of my cards."

"What were you doing here tonight?"

"As I told you, I'd been staying here last weekend, but somehow I left behind my sample case. I intended to have Wayne ship it to me, but after unsuccessfully trying to reach him the past few days, I decided to come after it myself. I still had a key, you see." She dug a key ring out of her purse. "It opens the kitchen door."

"How did you learn of Wayne Rival's death?"

"When my plane landed at SeaTac, I tried the number here first, then I called the Rival offices in Seattle. The woman who answered the phone told me."

Craig listened with growing disdain, certain the unseasoned police officers were buying the smelly hag's explanation as readily as they'd bought the rest of her fantasy. But he knew she was lying. If not, then why hadn't she tried contacting Wayne at the Seattle number before tonight? No. Rival Gems didn't do business with jewelry designers. The only association his befuddled brain could attach to Mesa, Arizona, was the DeHaviland family, who'd been pestering his father for years to sell them his grandmother's necklace from the Collection. But he couldn't conjure one memory of anyone named Carlyle. Damn! If only he could clear away the mist from his head....

Kaslow handed Lyssa her driver's license. "There are no signs of a forced entry. How did this man get into the house? Was the front door unlocked?"

"No. He used this key." Lyssa extracted the single key from her soggy pants pocket and presented it in the palm of her hand to the surprised police officers. "I found it when I searched his pockets. It m-must be the one Wayne kept hidden outside."

"Do you know for certain that Mr. Rival kept one hidden outside?"

"Yes. It was kept under a rock by the azalea bush next to the front door."

Kaslow went to check and was back a moment later. "There's no key there now. This must be the one."

Frustration flowed through Craig's veins. No! That key was his. He'd put it in his wallet when he left here last September and removed it when he'd arrived at the gate. Why did Officer Dunn believe everything that lunatic was telling him? If there was no sign of a break-in, then *she* must have taken the key kept outside. His need to convey this expressed itself in a futile groan.

Three consecutive sneezes followed. But they weren't his.

"Would it be all right if I used the shower and changed into some dry clothes?" Lyssa asked as she sneezed again.

"Do you have anything here?" Dunn asked.

"I'm sure I can find something of Wayne's. He wasn't much bigger than me."

"Then go ahead. Wouldn't want you to catch pneumonia."

PNEUMONIA WAS A DISTINCT possibility, Lyssa decided, heading for the master bedroom. As she passed through the living room, she wondered at the sheet-draped furniture, recalling the covered pieces in the foyer, as well. Wayne had died only three days ago, yet the house looked and felt as deserted as if he'd been gone a year or more. The master bedroom was the same. She stared at it in disbelief. Off and on over the past three months she'd slept in this room. It had become as familiar to her as her own bedroom in her little house in Mesa. Tonight she felt like an intruder here.

She hurried to the closet—to discover it was all but empty. Apparently whoever had closed the house had also packed up and taken away Wayne's clothes. She frowned. The few shirts and trousers now occupying these hangers looked like they'd fitted a man several inches taller than Wayne. She reached for one of the shirts, then spied an old gray sweatsuit and a pair of men's sneakers tucked on the floor, grabbing them up instead.

Fifteen minutes later her body was scrubbed clean, but she still felt cold and dirty on the inside, as though she'd done something to deserve the attack. She knew it was nonsense, a normal victim's reaction, but the feeling stayed with her as she tugged on the sweatsuit and threw her wet clothes into the washing machine.

To her relief, the ambulance had already taken the maniac away. Only Dunn remained behind, explaining that his partner had accompanied their prisoner to the hospital. He eyed Lyssa approvingly. "You look like a human being again."

Lyssa wiped at her nose with a tissue. "Yep. And I've got all the aches and pains and precold symptoms to prove it."

"Then, if you're ready, I'll take you to a motel in town."

One as far away from here as possible, she hoped. But what was she thinking? She couldn't leave. "No. Thanks. I mean, can't I stay here?"

"Well . . . I really shouldn't allow it."

Lyssa could see she'd have to persuade him. "Oh, please. What more could happen to me? I mean, you've got the bad guy. I don't think another will show up in his place. Besides, I'm certain Mr. Rival won't mind—after all, I've been a guest here so often I feel right at home." Her cheeks warmed, and Lyssa prayed the officer wouldn't see through her bluster.

Dunn grimaced. "I don't know. . . ."

"Ah, come on." She flirted shamelessly. Anything for Grandy. "Besides, my clothes are in the washing machine."

He considered a moment longer, then sighed. "Oh, I guess it'll be okay." He sauntered to the door. "We've parked the Cadillac inside the fence. A tow truck will be by sometime tomorrow to pick it up."

"Speaking of tow trucks, I wonder if you'd check on my car, take the keys and lock it? I'll have to call the airport rental place in the morning and see what they want done with it."

"Where exactly did you leave it?"

Lyssa shrugged. "Somewhere this side of the Tahuya River bridge. Near a stand of trees. You probably noticed it on the way here. It was the little Mazda hugging the big rock.''

''I'll keep my eyes peeled on the way back into town and see what I can do to secure it.'' Dunn opened the door and stepped onto the porch.

Lyssa watched the policeman walk down the driveway and through the gate. Then she closed and locked the front door. Leaning against its solid support, she drew a deep breath and let it out slowly. Despite her reassurances to Dunn, Lyssa wondered if she'd ever again feel safe alone.

Arguing with herself over the inanity of this feeling, she hurried through the kitchen and rechecked the back-door locks, lowered the blinds and turned off the lights. She stood in the darkened room listening for sounds of intruders, but heard only the hum of the refrigerator and the muted sloshing of the clothes washer. Nothing scary about that.

She knew she should call her mother and explain the delay, but Mom had worry enough with Grandy. Tomorrow she'd get another flight. Now she'd get Grandy's necklace. The only good thing about being alone was that she could go about the task without fear of being discovered.

Feeling a nudge of anticipation in the pit of her stomach, she headed straight for the library. The wall safe was hidden by a fifty-pound king salmon that had been mounted and hung above a Louis XIV-style desk. Her fingers trembled slightly as she swung the trophy fish toward her and caught hold of the safe's dial. During the past three months, she had put the necklaces in this safe each night and removed them each morning. *Please, let my Purity be here.*

Hearing the final click, Lyssa pulled the door open and peered into the compact cavern. Shocked disbelief poured through her achy body. The safe was empty.

What in the world had Wayne done with the necklaces?

Monday night she'd watched him put her Purity in the jeweler's case. Seconds later, she'd personally stuck the case in her carry-on bag and—except when Wayne had helped her load it into her car—kept the bag within reach. Distracted by worry for Grandy, she hadn't bothered to recheck the case, hadn't thought she'd had any reason to distrust Wayne...until the next day when she'd discovered the case was empty. The same incredulous fury she'd felt at that moment washed over her now.

Her mother had warned her about the Rivals. She should have listened. Lyssa slumped to the edge of the desk. On the other hand, remembering Wayne's kindness, she couldn't understand his reneging on their deal. Why let her make the faux, just to rob her of it? Not that it mattered now. What was done was done.

What did matter now was where he might have put the necklaces. Time had been on her side. Wayne hadn't lived long enough to take them anywhere else. Of course, there was always the off chance someone unknown had found them—perhaps the person responsible for the draped furniture—and absconded with them. That thought was too depressing to dwell on.

Anyway, she reasoned, Wayne had never liked putting the necklaces in the vault, protesting that any clever thief would look there first. Lyssa gazed around the den. Where else might he have put two such valuable pieces of jewelry? Anywhere. The possibilities in this room alone were staggering.

Rising stiffly, she left the library. Physical fitness was as much a part of Lyssa's life as her jewelry, but her body ached as though she hadn't exercised in years. The muscles in her calves and thighs felt like someone had shortened them when she wasn't looking.

She checked the time. Four hours before dawn. She was nearly asleep on her feet. Maybe she should go to bed. But what if Craig Rival caught her here? Lyssa shivered at the thought, but she could feel her body shutting down from tiredness. Two hours of sleep— what Dad called a power nap—would be enough. Then she'd be ready to go again, done and out of here, long before Craig Rival arrived.

Lyssa opened the door to the master bedroom and switched on the overhead light. The king-size bed seemed to beckon to her. Exchanging the overhead light for one of the bedside lamps, she shut the bedroom door and wedged a chair beneath the knob, then quickly checked the lock on the French doors that led to a private deck. Feeling more secure, she laid her wristwatch on the nightstand, curled into a ball on the bed and pulled the quilted spread over herself.

CRAIG WAS EXHAUSTED. He wished they would go away, all the people poking and prodding at him, asking questions he couldn't make sense of. Why wouldn't they let him sleep?

Officer Kaslow stood outside Craig's curtained emergency-room cubicle talking to a tall male doctor with thinning gray hair.

Dunn spotted his partner and strode to her side. "How's our prisoner?"

The doctor regarded them both with quizzical gray eyes. "Concussion. I'm Dr. Isaac Jones and I was just about to ask this officer why you've arrested Mr. Rival, and why he's been registered as a John Doe?"

"What?" Dunn exclaimed. "You mean that man *is* Craig Rival? Are you positive?"

"Of course I'm positive. I've known him all his life."

Kaslow regarded her partner with raised brows, then plucked the keys from Dunn's grasp. "We'd better get back to the Rival place, pronto."

LYSSA JERKED AWAKE. Shards of light from the bedside lamp poked her sleep-blurred eyes. Impatient to focus, she blinked rapidly, then gazed around the room. To her relief, she was still alone. The chair was still wedged firmly beneath the knob. But it was still dark. Her wristwatch confirmed that only an hour had passed since she'd lain down. What had awakened her?

Braced on one elbow, she listened. The house was as quiet as a graveyard at midnight. Five full minutes ticked off the digital watch before she snuggled under the bedspread and clamped her eyes shut.

A loud creak brought Lyssa sitting bolt upright. Someone was coming down the corridor. Her heart slammed against her rib cage. Surely the police hadn't let that maniac loose?

Footsteps stopped outside her room. The door-knob turned.

She leapt from the bed and vaulted to the door. "Wh-who's there?"

The doorknob rattled.

Horrified, Lyssa stuffed her feet into Wayne's spare sneakers, grabbed her purse and raced to the French doors. The thud of something hitting the door sent jolts of fear up her spine. Gingerly, she slipped outside, closing the French doors behind her. From inside, the persistent thumping continued. The petrifying noises hastened her exit over the deck railing. As Lyssa landed on the beach, she heard a different sound. The chair tumbling across the hardwood floor?

Chapter Three

Friday

"What are you doing here?" Craig Rival glanced in surprise at the man entering his hospital room, then continued to pull on his socks.

"It's nice to see you, too." David Lundeen, Rival's attorney, crossed the room with the grace of the long-distance runner that he was. Forty-something, David preferred black leather jackets and chino pants to pin-striped suits, and further chagrined his stodgy law partners—who happened to be his father and brothers—by moussing his white blond hair into faddish spikes like some highly paid professional athlete. "Stacey called, explained what happened, and I said I'd drive down and check into it."

Stacey was Wayne's daughter and the only person Craig had contacted. "Have you?"

"A little."

With a mixture of trepidation and hope, Craig asked, "Have they found the woman?"

"Nope, but after seeing what she managed to do to you, I'd say she's one clever customer."

Craig disliked the hint of a smile in the depths of his friend's blue eyes. He scowled at him, but received a huge grin in return. "Dammit, David. I don't find it a bit funny." He dropped his legs over the side of the bed and pulled on his rumpled slacks, hating the limp feeling of the unpressed lightweight wool against his freshly showered skin. "I've spent eight hours in this miserable place with my head pounding like a thumped melon, and you show up making jokes. Hand me that shirt."

"Excuse me. I didn't know you'd lost your sense of humor." David tossed the wrinkled item of clothing at Craig.

Craig grimaced, thoroughly chagrined. "All right, I'm sorry. I shouldn't take my frustration out on you."

David cocked his head. "Apology accepted. Are you sure you should be going home?"

"The doctor doesn't like it, but none of his arguments convinced me to stay put." Craig spent his lingering agitation on the shirt, ramming his arms into the disheveled silk sleeves and working the buttons with haste. It wasn't David's teasing that had irked him, it was his infernal worry for a woman he didn't even know—a woman with intense sea green eyes he couldn't get out of his mind.

"Ever since the police told me there really was someone trying to kill that woman . . ." He brushed at the smudges on his shirtfront. "I just want her found before it's too late." His fingers moved gingerly to his tender forehead. "Considering the hell she went through, I feel like a damned fool resenting her for this. Haven't they turned up any trace of her?"

David shook his head. "As I understand it, the minute Dr. Jones identified you, the police officers raced back to Windance, but the woman was gone."

"That's old news." Standing, Craig stuffed the unkempt shirttail into the equally untidy slacks and yanked the zipper shut. Lyssa Carlyle had caused him enough pain and anxiety to last a lifetime. Hell, he didn't even know what she looked like—wouldn't recognize her if she walked into this room. He owed her nothing. Why couldn't he shake the worry—no, the fear—he felt for the blasted woman? As quickly as he wondered, Craig realized he knew part of the answer. First his father, then Wayne. He couldn't bear the thought of a third tragic death associated with Windance. "Are you sure the police don't have anything new to report?"

David gaped at him. "I haven't checked in the last hour. I've had a few other items on my plate, such as helping to arrange the funeral—which takes place at eleven tomorrow morning, in case that bump you took knocked that fact from your brain—and worrying about my friend who's in the hospital with a concussion. The police's progress, or lack of it, is right near the bottom of my priority list. I know what you probably know—like I said, the woman was not at your house when the two officers returned. Her clothes, including her sneakers, were in your dryer. It's like she vanished into thin air. Frankly, I think whoever was after her came back and dragged her off somewhere."

"You've got a devious mind for someone who specializes in business law." But Craig's pulse surged unpleasantly. What David suggested had occurred to

Craig with sickening regularity during the last few hours. Granted he wasn't thinking as clearly as usual yet, but surely if her pursuer had come after the Carlyle woman at Windance there would have been some evidence of it. He slid his feet into his shoes, but kept his eyes on his friend. "You're wrong. Dunn and Kaslow told me the house was locked when they got back. They had to use my key to get in. They didn't find any signs of a break-in or a struggle."

"I know." David sighed loudly. "But why would the woman leave without her clothes?"

Craig couldn't answer that. He had a few other questions he couldn't answer, either. "What was she doing at Windance in the first place?"

"Beats me."

"Well, I'll feel better when I get home and check a few things out." Scooping up a comb, shaving cream and razor furnished by the hospital, Craig headed into the cubicle bathroom.

David followed and leaned against the jamb. A tolerant grin tweaked his full mouth. "Same old Craig...never take anything at face value."

Ignoring the gibe, Craig spread lather over his whiskers and studied the purple bruise above his left brow. Unbidden, Lyssa's image flooded his mind, presenting a surprisingly less-disgusting picture now that he knew the terror she must have experienced prior to their encounter. What did she look like beneath the grit and grime? Except for her unforgettable eyes, he hadn't a clue, and standing here all day wouldn't give him any. He scraped the razor under his chin. "Have you ever heard of this Lyssa Carlyle?"

David's eyes met Craig's in the mirror. "As a matter of fact, I have. She's a jewelry designer. Has a unique signature line and specializes in replicas of antique pieces. Real popular in several of Seattle's trendier shops. I've seen some of it. She's pretty good."

Craig watched shaving cream drip from his chin as this new information sank in. "She makes replicas of antique jewelry?"

"So? That's hardly a threat to Rival Gems."

"David, think about it. What would someone like Lyssa Carlyle want with a company that buys and sells antique and estate jewelry?"

The lawyer straightened. "The Collection?"

"I don't know. But it worries me."

"How would she get access to the Collection?"

Craig grew thoughtful. "Last night she told the police she was a business associate of Wayne's." He turned back to the mirror and attacked his angular face with the disposable shaver. Seconds later, he rinsed off the razor, discarded it in the wastebasket and regarded David over his shoulder. "Are you certain Wayne never mentioned her?"

"Positive." David tilted his head and narrowed his eyes. "Don't tell me you're thinking Wayne would let her copy the Collection pieces? That's nuts."

Craig knew David was right. Wayne wouldn't have allowed that. He dampened a washcloth and wiped the last of the lather from his smooth cheeks, wishing he could dispense of his thoughts of Lyssa Carlyle as easily. But he couldn't. He raked the comb through his thick black hair with a vengeance, then slid it into his pocket and slipped past David for a quick check of the room. The rapid movement made his head spin. "Well, if Wayne didn't tell her I was expected home today, who did? Dammit, two and two keep adding up to five."

David's brows lifted slightly and the delighted smirk was back. "She really got under your skin, didn't she, pal?"

An orderly pushing an empty wheelchair entered the room, saving Craig the necessity of denying the accusation. Lyssa Carlyle had certainly done more to him than knock him silly with a vase, but he didn't totally understand what. And the last thing he wanted right now was to dissect his jumbled feelings about the woman.

Craig sank into the wheelchair. "Let's go."

Outside, rain clouds huddled overhead like restless black sheep, and the air bristled with the smell of a coming storm. As they headed across the parking lot, a patrol car pulled up beside them. Officer Dunn emerged and approached Craig with an outstretched hand. "We found your rental car abandoned at the public boat launch." He handed Craig his jacket and his wallet. "It looks like the only thing missing is cash. Would you please confirm?"

Craig snatched the wallet from Dunn and immediately inspected the contents. Just as the policeman had said, the five-hundred cash he'd been carrying was gone. The stolen money was to be expected, but seeing his driver's license askew, and realizing a stranger had pawed through this private corner of his life, filled Craig with impotent rage. He wanted to put his fist through something solid, preferably the jerk's face.

He told Dunn about the missing money and asked about Lyssa Carlyle. Learning there was no sign of her, Craig insisted he be informed the minute there was, thanked the officer and settled himself in the passenger seat of David's Porsche.

David took his place behind the wheel, fastened his seat belt and started the engine. "I have some business in Olympia, but I'll be back to drive you to Seattle at around four."

Craig faced David. Did he really have business in Olympia? Or was he making himself scarce for a few hours because he knew Craig needed some time alone at Windance?

David drove out of the parking lot. "I've scheduled the reading of Wayne's will for seven Monday evening."

"Sure."

"In case Wayne didn't tell you, he was delighted that you made him a full partner. He was really excited about it."

Craig leaned back in the seat and sighed. "I never understood Granddad's logic. Wayne might not have been his natural son, but that was no reason to keep him from owning a share of the business. Wayne proved his worth."

"Too bad it was only for a week."

Craig grimaced, agreeing with David one hundred percent. He should have done it the minute he'd had the authority, but he'd been so grief stricken at the time, all he could think about was getting as far away from Washington as possible. Even then, it hadn't occurred to him until recently, and he deeply regretted the thoughtlessness of that. "Does anyone know what Wayne was doing at Windance the night he died?''

"Not that I've heard. I just assumed your imminent return was the reason for his visit." The corners of David's mouth tipped upward slightly. "He liked to pull random inspections, said he was keeping the caretaker honest."

A simple, logical explanation for Wayne's presence at Windance. Craig felt ashamed of doubting his uncle's character, even for a moment. He should have known there would be a good reason. Should have known he could trust Wayne implicitly.

As they turned onto the North Shore Road, Craig reexamined his violated wallet, scanning the photo section. Halfway through, his hand stayed. One of the cellophane sleeves was empty. A sinking feeling tugged at his gut, sucked at his heart. His voice come out hoarse with frustration. "Something else *is* missing. A picture of Dad, Wayne and me."

David turned incredulous eyes to him. "Are you sure the picture was there?"

"Yes. It's the only one of Dad I took with me to Europe."

Disquiet spattered inside his brain, as jarring as the first drops of rain hitting the windshield. Why would someone bent on murdering young women bother with a snapshot of three men he didn't even know?

RAINDROPS BEAT AGAINST the metal roof, jarring Lyssa from a fretful sleep. Momentarily disoriented, she raised her sore body to a sitting position on the musty divan. Of course…the Burleys' cabin. It looked more like a dump. She couldn't imagine anyone using this run-down rattrap as a pleasure retreat. But then, she wasn't here for pleasure, either. The reason she'd sought refuge here came back in a rush, speeding her heart rate. Evidently, she'd covered her forced entry well enough to fool her pursuer, but she wanted to make certain.

Lyssa hastened to the living room window, inched aside a dusty green drape and peered out.

Overhead, sinister black clouds pressed low, ready to explode into a full-blown thunderstorm. Rain hit the murky glass and dribbled in grimy streaks down the pane. The tide was low. Just how long had she been asleep? Instinctively, she glanced at her wrist, but the watch had been left behind. She had to get out of here. The Burleys had no telephone, and by now, Mom would be wondering what had happened to her.

The beach was deserted. Her gaze darted to the Rival house across the way. Was her pursuer lying in wait at Windance? The thought chilled her. It was Friday, around noon, she guessed. Surely, the police would notify Craig Rival of last night's break-in as soon as possible after his plane landed. If he decided to investigate, he could show up at Wayne's anytime now. She had to act quickly.

Stifling a sneeze, Lyssa tugged on the oversize sneakers she'd grabbed from Wayne's closet and caught hold of her purse with the back-door key to Windance tucked inside. Within minutes, she was on the beach, slogging across the sand as fast as she could manage. Wind and rain pelted her cheeks, tousled her long hair and dampened her rumpled sweatsuit. Lyssa didn't notice. She was running through her mental list. First, she'd use Wayne's phone to call her mother.

Second, she'd find the necklace. Third, she'd contact the police and answer their questions. Fourth, she'd make arrangements for the rental car and secure another. And fifth, she'd head home.

She crept across the deck and surveyed the driveway. Good. There were no cars either inside or outside the fence. Obviously the tow truck had come, taken the Cadillac and gone.

With her internal sensors on red alert, she let herself in, then stood immobile with her hand on the knob for one whole minute, straining to hear any sounds in the house. Finally, convinced she was alone, Lyssa headed for the telephone and dialed her mother's home number in Mesa.

Roxanne DeHaviland answered on the first ring, as though she'd been sitting beside the telephone willing this call. "Lyssa! Well, it's about time you got back. I've left half a dozen messages on your machine."

The worry in her mother's voice alarmed Lyssa. "Is Grandy worse?"

"No. The same—still critical. I think she's holding on to see the Purity, but who knows how long that will sustain her. Have you got it?"

"Not exactly."

"What does that mean?"

"I'm still in Washington."

"What? Is that rat Rival giving you a hard time about Grandy's wedding necklace?"

"Not exactly."

"Then what's wrong?"

What was right? "It's a long story, too long for now."

"I have all the time in the world, darlin' mine. Start talking." When she used this tone, Lyssa knew her mother's patience was thin.

Her own patience was dissipating rapidly. "Well, time is one luxury I don't have."

A sigh blew through the wire. "Then hit the highlights."

The roof of her mouth felt woolly. "Wayne Rival had a fatal heart attack Monday night shortly after I left for the airport."

"Whoa. No wonder you couldn't reach him." The *clank* of an earring against the receiver heralded Roxanne's next question. "What about the faux gem? Were you able to get it?"

"Not yet. But I will—within the hour." She wished she felt as confident as she sounded.

There was a pause on the other end of the line. Lyssa could almost see her mother's intent expression as the woman considered what she'd just been told. Then her mellow voice drifted through the line. "Nearly sixteen hours to track down the whereabouts of one necklace? What's taking so long?"

The memory of her pursuer sprang into her mind, and shivers burned across her flesh. There was no way she would broach this subject over the phone. "Let's save the gory details till I get home."

"Which will be...?"

"As soon as possible."

"I have the distinct impression that what you're holding back is more important than what you've told." The impatience in Roxanne's tone had been replaced by concern.

The woman was too shrewd at the moment. If Lyssa related her encounter with the maniac, her mother would have a stroke. And if her mother found out she had no idea where the wedding necklace was after telling Grandy she was bringing it to her, Lyssa would be the one needing a doctor. Thinking of her grandmother sent shards of worry through her. She said again, "I'll be there as soon as I can."

"The sooner, the better. I pray this stunt of yours works."

"It will." *If I can find the necklace.*

"Are you at that number in Belmont?"

"Yes. Why?"

"If Grandy takes a change for the worse, I'll call."

"No. I'll only be here a short while." *Please hang on, Grandy.* "I'll call you as soon as my plane touches Arizona soil."

"If I'm not here, I'll be at the hospital. Hurry home."

Lyssa dropped the receiver in its cradle, then stared at the telephone. *Home.* It was amazing how much one word could mean. She found her clothes in the dryer and changed. Heartened by the feel and fit of the familiar garments, she gladly dumped Wayne's into the hamper.

In the master bedroom, she found the bed had been smoothed, and the chair was now standing upright in its corner. The only sign that it had been violently forced from under the doorknob was a thin scratch in the oak veneer back and an almost invisible nick in one leg.

Her wristwatch was no longer on the bedside table. Nor anywhere else in the room. A fresh chill crossed her flesh. Someone had gone to great lengths to remove all evidence of her presence here. Why? The past few days had been like living through a nightmare. She urged aside this upsetting thought and started searching the room. There was no telling how much time she had before Craig Rival arrived.

Her noisy search through drawers and in closets and cupboards was drowned by the crescendo of raindrops hitting the roof and the thunder rattling the windows. The disconcerting orchestration hastened her hunt as effectively as the occasional flash of lightning behind the window shades suspended her heartbeat.

Lyssa had no idea how much time had passed, but the nerve-racking search was wearing her out. She'd found no trace of the missing necklaces. If they were in this house, they weren't in the bedrooms. She headed into the living room and contemplated the shrouded furnishings. The wind wailed against the house like a tortured creature crying for mercy, and for the first time in her long ordeal, she felt as though she might break down and cry, too.

A sudden lull in the storm coincided with the sound of a key in the front door. Blood froze in Lyssa's veins. Panic climbed into her throat. Then she realized it had to be Craig Rival. The maniac didn't know her whereabouts. Just the same, she couldn't be found here by Wayne's nephew. He'd toss her out on her ear, and she'd never retrieve her grandmother's necklace.

The door swung open, and she hit the floor behind the sofa, slipping the sheet over herself.

CRAIG DROPPED HIS suitcase and a tiny grocery sack to the floor, shook the rain from his hair like a wet dog and kicked the door shut. Whatever David's reason for making himself scarce, he was glad to be alone. Before he left for the funeral, Craig wanted to reacquaint himself with Windance.

He let his gaze roam the entryway. Confirmation of Lyssa Carlyle's attack on him remained clearly in evidence: the sheet that had covered the trestle table and antique bench heaped against the floorboards; the swept-up pile of broken Dresden vase in the corner. Ironically, someone had returned the throw rug to its rightful place.

An image of Lyssa Carlyle flashed into his mind again, highlighted by her arresting eyes. It startled him, giving rise to a wealth of irrational emotions. What was it about this woman that he couldn't get her out of his mind? Why did he long to see her again, to talk to her, to know that she was safe?

The storm battered the house, sending a chill to his bones. He switched on the electric thermostat and moved into the living room. The window shades blocked his view of the wicked weather and cast spectral shadows over the sheet-clad furniture. Craig drew a deep breath, refamiliarizing himself with the special scent of his lifelong home. He could almost swear that he smelled the faint, lingering aroma of . . . sea monster.

Oddly enough, however, there was not the damp, musty smell he would have expected in a beach house that had been closed for a year. It appeared someone *had* used the house in his absence, as Ms. Carlyle claimed. If not Wayne, then who? Stacey?

Deciding to check his utility bills the first chance he got, Craig strode across the room and adjusted the shades one by one, until all five plate-glass windows were uncovered and the storm was in full view.

Lyssa cowered against the couch, afraid to breathe. Dust tickled her nose. She felt a sneeze building and struggled to stifle it.

Craig stared at the violent waves and thought of another September day on the canal, a day of warm blue skies and slate-smooth water, a day for father and son to strengthen their bond. A perfect day, until his father had drowned.

God, how he missed his dad. He shoved away from the windows and began stripping the sheets from the furniture.

Chapter Four

A woman huddled behind the sofa, gaping up at Craig.

Craig jolted back, his heart skipping dangerously. "What the—?"

Strands of the woman's long golden hair stood out, static-charged from the friction of the sheet. Horror spread across her face.

Those sea green eyes. Lyssa Carlyle! What in the hell was she doing back in his home?

Before he could ask, she leapt to her feet, screaming and swinging her fists, swatting aside his attempts to grab her. She still thought he was the maniac who'd tried to kill her. "Wait! I'm not—"

Her knee rocketed toward his groin. Craig jerked back. The blow landed off center. Craig grunted, doubling over.

Lyssa ran for the foyer.

Clumsily, Craig followed. "Ms. Carlyle! I'm not the one who tried to kill you!"

She kept running. She charged through the foyer into the kitchen and grasped the doorknob just as Craig caught up to her. He snapped his arms crisscrossed over her upper torso, locked his hands above his wrists and hauled her roughly to him.

She fought like a rabid squirrel, kicking and shrieking.

"I'm not going to harm you in any way. I promise. I'm Craig Rival. And this time I have my wallet to prove it."

The thunderstorm outside was less fierce than the conflict inside. Lyssa's continued struggles told Craig he wasn't getting through to her. Shock, no doubt.

Fearing he was bruising her, Craig nonetheless bundled her back to the living room and dropped her onto the sofa. They were both breathing hard. The exertion had started his head pounding with a devilish drumbeat. Ignoring it, Craig plopped on top of her, straddling her legs with his, pinning her beneath him, clamping her wrists over her head with one hand. She bucked, trying to throw him. Her ear-shattering scream snapped his control. "Shut up!" He reached behind him to grab his wallet from his pants pocket.

Taking advantage, Lyssa lurched to her left, pulling him off-balance. Craig swore, then yanked her back to an upright position and rammed his driver's license under her nose. "Look. See what it says? Craig Rival."

Blinking with terror, her lungs struggling to pull in tiny chirps of breath, Lyssa stared at the license. The words swam before her eyes. Five seconds passed before the name registered. Craig Rival. She gazed from the man to the picture. Three times. It was one of the few flattering auto license photographs she'd ever seen, and it left absolutely no doubt—the handsome man pinning her to the couch was Craig Rival, Wayne's nephew.

Her heartbeat faltered and her breath hitched as she lifted her gaze to Craig. There wasn't a fleck of murderous intent or innate madness in his black-brown eyes. Only concern and compassion. Reality hit her like a gust of cold wind; this man hadn't tried to kill her. A dry sob racked her, then another and another, until she was overcome with them.

With a relieved sigh, Craig felt the rigidity drain from his tensed muscles. He released her and retreated to the cushion beside her, then pulled her close, gently this time. Her body seemed all loose bone as she slumped against him. "I know, I know. You've had a hell of a time. But you're safe now."

Safe. Yes, safe. Like a drowning woman who'd been thrown a life preserver, Lyssa suddenly grabbed for him, tunneling her arms beneath his jacket. She encircled his lean waist and dug her fingers into the folds of his silk shirt as she burrowed her head against his muscled chest. In the security of his embrace, with his erratic heartbeat thrumming in her ears, she sobbed, letting out the fear and anger and relief that flowed forth like an untapped gusher.

Resting his chin on her head, Craig stroked her heaving back and caressed her sun-streaked hair. Gone was the sea monster stench. She smelled of shampoo and felt as helpless and vulnerable as a child, a child fate had thrust into his unwilling care. And yet a part of him was not reacting to her in a fatherly way, by any stretch of the imagination. What was it about her? He didn't know Lyssa Carlyle from Eve. Hell, he suspected her of the worst kind of duplicity, but even that didn't lessen this almost obsessive concern he'd had for her since she'd cracked him on the head.

He shifted his hands across her back protectively, disturbed by the intangible bond he felt forming between himself and this woman. It wasn't something he could hold in his hands and examine. Nonetheless it was as real as the Hope diamond—and he understood at least a part of it was rooted in the trauma they had shared, that terrifying, equalizing experience.

Lyssa's sobs quieted to a soft mewling, but she made no attempt to disengage herself. Apparently the close contact was somehow comforting her. Craig had to admit being needed like this, if even momentarily, felt damned good.

It was amazing. In less than twenty-four hours, what he'd been through because of this woman had done for him what a whole year in Europe hadn't: it made him care whether or not he was alive. Even the thought of Wayne's funeral tomorrow no longer filled him with dread. Yes, he was alone, but he didn't have to be lonely.

Through the picture windows, he watched distant lightning bolts stab the choppy water. The storm was passing. He felt Lyssa's shoulders quaver, heard her weary sigh and knew the storm inside her was also abating.

He looked down. She was gazing up at him with those incredible eyes that reminded him of hot, lazy nights on the shores of the Mediterranean. His pulse skittered. She wore absolutely no makeup and, though her nose was red and her eyes and mouth slightly swollen from crying, she was not in the least unattractive.

In fact, just the opposite.

Her mouth was pouty, the bottom lip fuller than the top, her nose narrow, straight, her eyes round, large— her best feature. She looked more teenager than woman, definitely not the sophisticated type he invariably preferred, and yet there was no denying she had his heart beating faster.

LYSSA PULLED HER GAZE from Craig's and shoved herself from his embrace. She knew she ought to be highly embarrassed, clinging to him—a Rival, of all people—but she wasn't. Not in the least.

Then, for the first time, she noticed his dirty shirt-front and the sickening purple bruise on his forehead. All she had done and said to this man, from their first encounter until now, was replayed in a rush—the crack on his head, tying him up, having him arrested, knee-ing him.... The embarrassment she'd denied a moment ago attacked full force. Her face burned and she drew her hands to her mouth. "You must hate me. I'm so sorry. Are you all right?"

Craig's grin was lopsided, endearing. "You pack quite a wallop, but the doc says I'll be good as new in a week or so."

"I could have killed you," she whispered, horrified at the realization.

"It'll take more than a Dresden vase to crack open my thick skull."

Lyssa winced, guessing from the amused glint in his dark eyes that he was teasing her, using her own words to lighten the tension between them. "If it makes you feel any better," Craig said, gently moving a strand of her hair off her cheek, "in your place I'd have reacted much the same."

It didn't make her feel better at all; she could have caused him permanent damage. However, he did look and sound sincere. Probably just being polite. Then again, why should he be? In spite of her scorn for the Rivals, she felt her bond with Craig tighten a notch. She owed him so much—the least of which was an explanation. "They—they came back...whoever was after me...after the police took you away."

Remembering how he'd denied this, Craig realized now that it was the only scenario that made any sense. "That's what we feared when your clothes were still in my dryer." Craig touched the sleeve of her sweater, vaguely recalling that the one she'd worn the night before had been a dingy red. This was obviously the same sweater, clean. He lifted his gaze to her face. "Did you see the man? Can you describe him for the police?"

Lyssa shook her head, remembering the figure in the raincoat and hat, remembering her inability to tell if it was a man or a woman. "No."

"That's all right." Craig was struck with a sense of awe at the courage this woman possessed, at what it must have taken for her to return to this house. But what had brought her back? Surely it was more than the need to retrieve an oversize sweater and a pair of denims with ripped knees. The urge to ask was strong, but he sensed he'd better take it slow. "How did you get away?"

Wringing her hands, Lyssa rapidly filled him in on the night of horror she'd somehow survived.

"The police suggested something similar," he informed her, impressed that she'd had the presence of mind, despite her terror, to escape.

"Then you've spoken to the police this morning. H-have they caught whoever was after me?"

Craig pressed his lips together, hating having to tell her, then finally admitted, "No."

She shuddered, hugging herself against a fresh onslaught of shivers.

There were a dozen questions he wanted to ask, but not while she was still shaky. He ought to call the police, let them know she was alive and well, but that too would have to wait. He was going to have his answers first, before the police took over. Craig stood, the ache in his head now only a dull hum, and extended his hand. "Come on. I picked up some coffee and soup on the way home. I'm starving, and I'll bet you haven't eaten anything today."

Lyssa realized he was right. She had had a snack on the plane Thursday afternoon, but nothing since. She took his hand, expecting his brotherly concern to feel brotherly, but as she placed her callused hand into his much smoother, much larger, and definitely much warmer one, she was unprepared for the almost electrical shock that raced up her arm.

He retrieved a small brown paper bag from next to his suitcase and led her into the kitchen to the table that occupied the bay window. Craig removed his jacket and dropped it onto a chair. Rolling up his shirtsleeves, he said, "Sit."

Lyssa stared at his strong, tanned forearms, which were lightly furred with black hair. Disconcerted by her awareness of this man, she tugged her gaze away and settled into the chair with the best view of the canal, the chair which over the past few months she'd come to think of as her own special one.

First thing in the morning and on work breaks, she'd sought this spot, watching the ever-active wonders of nature and feeling a soul-warming peace. Not now. Lyssa gazed out the window at the clearing sky and the smoothing water and felt like an alien in a world that only a week before had been her second home. How could one week make such a difference?

The mouth-watering smells of coffee and clam chowder intruded on her somber musing, once again drawing her attention to Craig. She was glad that handsome face didn't belong to a psycho, and was finding it harder by the moment to comprehend that she'd ever thought it could. But it was most difficult to imagine that Wayne and he had been uncle and nephew. There was not a shred of family resemblance. Wayne had been slight of build with hazel eyes and classic Scandinavian features, whereas Craig's olive skin, his blue-black hair and regal nose hinted at Spanish ancestry.

Her gaze roamed his long, lean body, and she wondered how she could ever have thought it average. Although his clothes were creased and soiled, there was no mistaking the cut and quality, nor the fact that he appeared comfortable in business attire; the guys she knew would have changed into sweatsuits to cook. Not Craig. She had no trouble picturing him in a penthouse in Seattle with a panoramic view of Puget Sound, the hustle and bustle of the city providing the background music to the dynamic life he undoubtedly loved. Lyssa rolled her shoulders and thought about her own little house in Mesa, surprised that she didn't miss it. She'd spent most of the summer here, walking the beach, warm sand squishing between her bare toes and, until last night, she had grown to love the smell of salt water in her nose. Had even—now that her business was taking off—seriously considered relocating to one of the coastal cities, so she could build her own Windance.

After last night, the idea was less appealing.

But what about Windance? Did it really belong to Craig, not Wayne? Recalling it now, she realized Wayne had always seemed out of place here. She couldn't say the same of Craig; he wielded that wooden spoon as if he'd prepared more than one meal in this kitchen, and there was something about him as sturdy as the umber-tiled countertops, as bright as the chrome-topped stove and as natural as the hardwood floors.

No, this man was not average. Men like Craig Rival stood out in crowds, possessing a magnetism that even rumpled clothing and domestic chores couldn't conceal. She didn't doubt he drew women like...like Kevin did.

The thought of her ex-husband brought Lyssa lurching to her feet, scraping back her chair.

The noise caught Craig's attention. He turned toward Lyssa. Her face was pale again. He watched her cross to a bank of drawers and reach inside as though she knew this was where the silverware was kept. Again, questions of her familiarity with his house begged to be asked. His hand gripped tighter on the wooden spoon. Patience, he warned himself. She was still too distressed, probably still thinking about her ordeal.

Lyssa was still thinking about Craig...and Kevin. She removed silverware from the drawer, then went to the dish cupboard and brought Craig two cups and two bowls. He was looking at her oddly, his expression almost chagrined.

Who knew what men like him thought about? For the past three years she had purposely avoided his type. Handsome men. Granted, Craig wasn't a male model like Kevin, but most good-looking men had egos a mile wide that needed constant stroking from women. Lots of women. The image of Kevin in bed with her cousin darted into her mind, and Lyssa's empty stomach pitched. Damn. The memory could still spoil her appetite. Not because she harbored any tender feelings for Kevin. She didn't. But she never wanted to fall in love with another man who was even remotely like him.

Tamping down the old resentment, Lyssa returned to her chair. Was it only Craig Rival's handsome face that reminded her of Kevin? She set the spoons in place, thinking that something else had brought her ex-husband to mind. Something about Windance? Or Wayne? Something she ought to remember, but couldn't.

Well, perhaps it was just Craig and his wild good looks that had triggered the comparison. She put a napkin in her lap. Why should she care if Craig was a lady-killer? She'd only just met the man. It couldn't matter. But...somehow it did. This was crazy. Disastrous. The Rivals and the DeHavilands had been at odds for years. They had only one thing in common, and although it was a part of each of their family histories, their mutual desire for the Purity would never make them allies.

Craig seemed to study her as he filled the bowls with chowder, the cups with coffee. He made two trips to the table, then finally sat opposite her. Almost immediately, her queasiness was conquered by the delicious aromas.

Craig carried the conversation, keeping it light, comparing the richness of European cuisine with his canned clam chowder. He was rewarded by seeing her relax as she ate.

Lyssa gave into the fortifying powers of the hot food, letting Craig's soothing voice and his reassuring presence erase the final chill from her body. Draining her coffee cup, she extended it to be refilled, surprised to find herself smiling. It seemed a long time since she'd smiled. "You're not a bad cook."

"Coffee and soup." Craig grinned mockingly, noting how her face seemed lighted from the inside when she smiled, and poured more coffee into his own cup, as well. "Specialties of the house, Ms. Carlyle."

"We've shared too much to be so formal, Craig." She eased back in her chair and crossed her tired legs at the ankles. "Please, call me Lyssa."

"All right," he answered. She appeared relaxed, open. He'd suppressed his impatience to the bursting point. Craig hoped she was as ready to explain as he was to listen. "Now that we're on a first-name basis, I wonder if you'd satisfy my curiosity?"

"I'll try." Lyssa's guard shot up, pulling her straighter in her chair.

The reflex wasn't lost on Craig. He'd wanted to trust her, but he didn't know this woman, and no matter how much they might have bonded, that bond didn't ensure her honesty. He shifted in his chair and leaned his arms onto the table. "What were you doing in my house last night and again today?"

Chapter Five

Lyssa felt the heat flushing her cheeks. The moment she told him who she was, he would hustle her out of here so fast her head would spin. "I, uh, I left something here."

Craig frowned. "When? Last night?"

"Last . . . Monday night."

His frown deepened into a scowl that upscaled the ache at his temples. "Last—?"

"That's right." She cut him off, talking as fast as a high-pressure salesperson. "When I returned home, I discovered I'd left something of value here. Don't you remember me telling the police that I came to get it?"

Craig tapped a finger against his coffee cup, an angry drumming, and spoke so deliberately the muscles in his throat strained. "I remember you telling the police several things, like my uncle giving you a key to this house."

At least he remembered that. Lyssa felt the pressure on her chest ease a modicum. "He did."

"I didn't believe that last night and I don't believe it now."

"Well . . . well, I can prove it." She popped up and hurried from the room. A moment later she was back, digging a key ring from a filthy purse. She tugged a key loose and handed it to Craig.

He eyed it suspiciously, unimpressed.

She knew he was thinking she'd taken it from outdoors, but the hidden key outside fit the front door. "It opens the kitchen door."

Craig jerked his head toward her. His jaw clamped. Disquiet stirred deep inside him. Damn. It did look like the key he'd given Wayne, but his uncle wouldn't have let a complete stranger stay at Windance. Would he? Craig drank more coffee, thinking it tasted as weak as his confidence in his uncle. Grimly, he rose and tried the key.

The quiet click told him he hadn't known his uncle as well as he'd thought.

He returned to the table, angry—at Wayne for not living up to his image of him, and at this woman for causing the disillusionment. "I think you'd better tell me how my uncle came to give you this. And just how the hell you came to be leaving anything in my house."

Lyssa blanched, hearing Wayne's warning in her head as clearly as if he were standing beside her shouting it. *"Craig will be furious if he finds out about the Purity."*

And he certainly did look furious. There was little doubt he'd blow a gasket when he knew who she was. For a minute, she considered appealing to his sentimental side. Maybe family was as important to him as it was to her. Maybe he would understand how much she loved her grandmother. How much the wedding necklace meant to a dying woman whose family hadn't seen one lasting marriage since the day the necklace was sold to the Rivals. Her palms were damp. Maybe he didn't have a sentimental side. Maybe he'd laugh at her.

Resolve hardened inside Lyssa. Grandy was counting on having the Purity in her possession again, holding it again, and while there was still a breath of a chance to find the copy she'd made, Lyssa couldn't afford to be hustled off the premises. Even if it meant lying. "Wayne told me *he* owned Windance. I came here as his guest."

"Guest?"

"Yes." Maybe *guest* was stretching it, but that was what she'd claimed and now she was stuck with it. She took a bracing swallow of coffee, then blurted out a hastily devised lie. "I, uh, met Wayne at a jewelers' convention in Seattle, about six months ago. We just . . . you know, hit it off. One thing led to another and we . . . we started seeing one another. Spending weekends here."

Craig's coffee eyes darkened. "Without exception, Uncle Wayne liked his women redheaded, creamy-skinned and top-heavy. You want to try the truth this time?"

An inhaled breath lodged like a lump of sand in her throat. His expression was as cold as his voice, and Lyssa suspected he already knew the truth. Or a part of it. But which part? Her connection to the De-Havilands? Could the police have unearthed that information since last night? Maybe not, but it was only a matter of time. She licked her dry lips with an equally dry tongue. "I'm sorry I lied. It isn't something I usually do."

Certain he'd never believe that now, she stammered, "Wayne told me you would not approve of what went on between us, and I..." Great. This sounded worse. She blushed again, hating the unfamiliar heat that kept attacking her with ever-increasing regularity. She wasn't a blusher by nature. But her emotions were too raw, too easily triggered, she realized, struggling to rouse some of her usual poise. "There was nothing personal about our relationship. I contacted Wayne and put a proposition to him which he agreed to."

"What kind of proposition?"

Nose to nose with the moment of truth, Lyssa decided to lay it all on the line. Her hands were trembling. "My mother's maiden name is DeHaviland."

Craig's eyes widened.

"Before you ask, yes, I am related to Harland DeHaviland, the designer and original owner of the Purity, and yes, my proposition had to do with the necklace."

With the necklace. Singular. Not *the Collection.* Craig felt not an ounce of relief. "What proposition?"

Lyssa ignored his intimidating glare and plunged on. "I make antique replicas—"

"The proposition." he repeated.

Lyssa squared her shoulders and lifted her chin. "Since you wouldn't allow my family to buy the Purity, I decided the next best thing would be to make a copy of it."

"And you expect me to believe that Wayne allowed that?"

Lyssa could see he did believe it. He just didn't like it. "Wayne said you'd object."

"Damn right I do!"

"Why?"

"Because the value of any unique item is diminished when it's copied."

"Phooey! There is a whole group of consumers out there who like antique jewelry but can't afford the *unique* prices your pieces bring." Lyssa noticed his face had turned an unattractive red. Given his recent concussion, she'd bet his head was throbbing. "Look, do you want some aspirin or something?"

"No. I'd like you to continue."

This was one stubborn man. "I didn't make an exact copy. I used zircons." She shrugged. "What else do you want to know?"

He lowered his eyelids and rubbed his temples with his fingertips. Maybe he should have accepted her offer of aspirin. His head felt close to imploding.

Lyssa sipped her coffee, wondering if she was going to have to call the doctor. He didn't look at all well.

Ten seconds passed. Craig shook his head and assessed her with an intense gaze. "I want to know why. Why didn't you make an exact copy of the Purity? Why a faux worth a quarter or less of the real thing?"

"I told you. That's not what I do."

"But you said you wanted the Purity back in your family, so I'm assuming you have no intention of making it available to that whole group of consumers you mentioned. Why the faux?"

Lyssa realized she'd counted on his headache to chase this little detail from his mind. No such luck.

She admitted grudgingly, "All right. You're right. I don't want a faux Purity for my family." Her great-great-grandfather had that necklace made for her great-great-grandmother, Purity Arness. The necklace was her wedding gift from her groom and was named after her. Nothing less than the real thing would suit Lyssa. "But I'm hoping it will suit Grandy."

"Grandy?"

"Idella DeHaviland, my maternal grandmother. The necklace was supposed to be hers on her wedding day. Instead it went to your grandmother. Grandy has never gotten over it. She thinks not having the wedding necklace was responsible for the failure of her marriage, my parents' marriage and my own marriage."

His eyebrows shot up in disbelief.

"I didn't say I believed it. But Grandy does. As far back as I can remember, she's had this obsession. I suppose she's never forgiven her father for the foolish investments he made that forced the sale of their estate and everything in it, including her necklace. Grandy is eighty-three. Since the first of the year, her health has been failing rapidly. I made the faux in hopes of giving her some peace of mind."

"Surely she'll know the difference."

"I don't think so. My copy is excellent," Lyssa said without modesty. "Besides, given her condition, her diminished eyesight and the fact that she hasn't seen the Purity since she was eighteen, I felt the risk was worth taking."

Craig tipped his head back and stared at the ceiling for a long moment, then leveled his unnerving gaze at her. "If Wayne let you make your copy, why are you here?"

"Your uncle insisted on secrecy and only agreed to my proposition if I would do the work here. I finished the faux Monday afternoon and flew to Mesa with it. But somehow Wayne relieved me of it as he was helping me load my things into the car. So I came back to confront him. I need that faux. But I can't find either of the necklaces."

"Necklaces?"

"Of course. I had to have the real Purity here to make the copy."

The thought of the Purity being in this unsecured place alarmed Craig. He warned himself not to dwell on it, not to get sidetracked again. "Are you saying that Wayne stole your faux and hid it at Windance?"

Lyssa sighed, sitting straighter in the chair. "Yes. As near as I can figure, Wayne suffered that heart attack within half an hour of my departure for the airport. He wouldn't have had time to remove the necklaces. They have to be here somewhere."

Craig closed his eyes against the pain in his head and the new accusations. It was unbelievable. First Wayne allowed the copy, then he stole it? Why? Would Wayne really strike such a deal with a DeHaviland? After he'd made Wayne a full partner? He opened his eyes and stared at Lyssa. She flinched as if he'd touched her with more than his gaze. He reminded himself she only *looked* childlike, and that was due to her lack of makeup and that free-flowing golden hair that a man could bury his hands and face in.

But was she as innocent as she looked? Maybe she was lying again—as she had about Wayne and her being lovers. Maybe before he condemned his uncle, he needed more proof than a kitchen key. "So, you came back for your faux Purity, but you can't find it?"

"No. I haven't looked everywhere yet, but—" Something in his expression stopped her.

Craig felt a kernel of justification. "How do I know there *is* a faux Purity? For that matter, how do I know you even have a grandmother?"

Lyssa stiffened, indignant. "You can call Saguaro County General."

"I'll just do that." Craig rose, ignoring the wave of dizziness that immediately swept him, went to the telephone on the counter and called long-distance information. He scribbled the number on a tablet, then dialed. "What did you say her name was?"

Lyssa carried the dirty dishes to the sink. "Idella DeHaviland. You'll want the cancer center," Lyssa answered, speaking the word *cancer* in a low voice, as if saying it louder would somehow lend the disease more power against her grandmother.

Craig's heart went out to her. His mother also had had cancer, and he knew the devastation of watching a loved one slowly wither and die. He shook away the brutal memories. "What kind of cancer?"

It was none of his damned business, and yet he couldn't stop himself from asking. It was as if their bond kept winding tighter around them.

"Breast cancer. But it's spread."

"I'm sorry."

She nodded, looking as if she'd choke on any reply. Craig set the receiver in the cradle, then lifted it again and dialed a local number. He spoke, listened, then spoke again. "Officer Dunn. Craig Rival calling. Yes,

I see. I'm sorry he hasn't been caught, but I have good news for you. Ms. Carlyle turned up here. Safe and sound. No, no charges. Certainly. Here.'' He handed the phone to Lyssa. ''He wants to talk to you.''

Craig left her alone to give her statement.

Ten minutes later, he returned wearing a white dress shirt and crisp jeans that she recognized from the collection of clothing she'd seen in the master bedroom closet. He smelled of Eternity cologne. His dark hair was damp, swept off his forehead. Despite the purplish bruise, he looked as handsome in this casual wear as he had in the rumpled suit. More so. And just as comfortable. Another thing he had in common with Kevin. It probably explained her attraction to him. For she couldn't deny she was attracted to him, in spite of her promise to herself about gorgeous men—and this one a Rival. Her mother would have a fit.

Suddenly self-conscious about her own appearance, she realized her hair hadn't seen a brush in two days, and without her usual touch of mascara and lipstick she probably looked as faded as her jeans, if not as ill-treated. She scrounged in her purse and came up with a tube of lip balm, but no lipstick.

''You satisfy Dunn's curiosity?'' Craig asked.

''Yes. He wants me to come to the station, sign a statement and collect the stuff they retrieved from my banged-up rental car.''

''My lawyer is picking me up at four. We'll drop you off.''

''Good. I've arranged for another car with an agency in town.''

He nodded, then hesitated a moment, seeming to search for words that didn't come easily. ''I've been thinking. If you can find your faux Purity before David arrives, you can have it. I'll even help you search.''

Lyssa couldn't believe his generosity. Especially since she could see he wasn't wholly convinced there was a faux. Perhaps he needed to see it to believe it. In any case, he'd have been justified in insisting she call a taxi and get out of his life, and, given Wayne's description of him, and her mother and Grandy's opinion of the Rivals in general, that was exactly what she'd expected. But Craig Rival was proving a surprise on all counts.

For the next two hours, they covered the house thoroughly, but as it became clear the search would yield nothing, she could feel her credibility slipping away. Craig likely thought she was a liar or a thief or both, and arguing the point without proof to the contrary would only waste breath. By the time David Lundeen arrived, the silence between them was as grim as the day.

On the drive to Belmont, Lyssa sat jammed in the tiny back seat, which was more of a shelf, in the flashy Porsche, listening to the two men converse in low tones about people she didn't know. Her Purity was gone. All that hard work for nothing. Grandy would be heartbroken. She was heartsick. But there wasn't a blessed thing she could do about it.

The car came to a sudden stop, halting her thoughts. They were parked outside the Belmont Police Station. Craig hustled from the car and helped her out, as if he couldn't get rid of her soon enough.

But when he took her hand, unwanted sensations tingled deep within her, and although he might not think much of her as a person, his eyes told her he clearly felt something for her as a woman. Lyssa cringed inside, helpless to change the situation, or the circumstances that had brought them together and that held them apart. "Thank you for...everything. I'll expect a bill for the vase."

"Not necessary." He looked as though the thought of further contact with her was disconcerting.

"Yes, it is," Lyssa insisted, a sudden gush of optimism spurting through her. He hadn't heard the last of her. What if Grandy went into another remission? She had done so once already. It could happen again. There might be time to make another copy. *If* she could overcome the obstacle of Craig Rival. "The hospital bill, too."

"Just be safe," he said with a seriousness that surprised her.

She gazed into his eyes, wondering who she was trying to reassure more, and said, "Believe me, staying safe is my top priority."

Would she be safe? Craig wondered as she quickly stepped back and hurried away. The fact that he cared jarred him. Lyssa Carlyle, née DeHaviland, was no longer his responsibility. Hell, she'd never been his responsibility. Only unfortunate circumstances had brought them together. He wouldn't be seeing her again. He felt an odd twinge of disappointment at the realization.

But he knew he was better off. He didn't like mysteries. He liked facts—solid, hold-in-his-hands, see-with-his-own-eyes facts. She was all trust-me-I'm-telling-you-the-truth. His hand slid through his hair, ruffling it. But what was the truth? He watched her disappear into the building, and wished his brain were generating with all its cylinders.

David honked the horn impatiently. Craig hurried to the car. Worry niggled at him, but try as he might, he couldn't conjure any source for it.

An hour and a half later the Seattle skyline came into view; the city seemed larger, taller, more cosmopolitan than Craig remembered, but maybe it had always been this way and he just hadn't noticed. He felt an anxious tug in his chest as David maneuvered onto the Madison Avenue exit and turned left, driving down the sloping hillside toward Elliot Bay.

Craig's head had cleared, his worry focused. Despite not finding the necklace, Lyssa Carlyle had conducted herself during their search as if she expected to find it. If he believed her story, he'd have to believe that the Purity had been at Windance last Monday night, at the time of Wayne's heart attack. So, did he believe her story? His palms were damp, and the jumping in his gut wouldn't ease until he set eyes on the Purity, until he held it.

One block from the waterfront, David parked at the rear entrance of a redbrick warehouse, in an alley that ran north and south and connected Madison and Spring Avenues. Until ten years ago the building had sat vacant, then an innovative contractor had seen its potential, renovated it and leased spaces to a number of businesses, including the suites where Rival Gems International bought and sold estate jewelry.

"Sure you wouldn't rather go straight to the condo?" David asked. "You look pretty beat."

"I'm fine. I want to see the place." The Collection was what he really wanted to see. Immediately. He stepped from the car and leaned toward David's open window. "Afterward, I promise I'll catch a cab and head straight for my bed. See you tomorrow. And, Dave...thanks."

He straightened and drew in a breath as the car roared away. The air was cool, rife with the briny scent of the bay and impending rain. Black clouds pressed low, enforcing an early darkness. The roar of late afternoon traffic seemed to say, "Hurry, Craig, hurry."

He hastened inside, then turned right toward the elevator, barely aware of the teal carpet cushioning his footfalls, the mellow ecru walls, the greasy odor of deep-fry oil wafting from the Asian fast-food café at the end of the hallway.

Minutes later, the elevator arrived at the fourth floor. Craig stared at the redbrick wall with the five-inch brass letters proclaiming Rival Gems International. At least this hadn't changed, he thought with relief. He shoved through the solid mahogany door beside the lettering. Would the Purity be missing from the Collection case, as he feared?

With his heart beating erratically, he stepped into the windowless anteroom and passed the two unoccupied leather chairs to the inside door, knowing an interior chime had alerted anyone in the showroom or offices of his arrival.

Permeated by anxiety, he unlocked the door and hurried inside. The overhead light was brilliant. Windows, strategically placed in the old brick walls, added to the glare. Rival Gems had occupied this suite of offices for the past ten years. The carpets were mauve, the chairs and stools mahogany and navy blue leather. Brass and glass abounded.

Like the anteroom, the showroom was unoccupied. No one came to stop him as he all but ran to the alcove at the far wall, to the case displaying the Collection.

Craig's heart nearly leapt from his chest at the sight that met him. The whole case was empty.

Chapter Six

"The last flight to Phoenix left an hour ago. The next earliest is tomorrow." The airline clerk fiddled with his computer. "Let me check availability."

Lyssa sighed in frustration as the clerk related that all the morning and afternoon flights were full. Her options came down to standby or an evening flight. She took the sure thing, presented her credit card, secured the ticket and extended the lease on her rental car. Hoisting her nearly empty carry-on bag, she wandered through the stream of travelers arriving at and leaving SeaTac International, until she spotted a bank of telephones. Reluctantly, she dialed her mother's number and was relieved when the answering machine responded; explanations about her delay needed telling in person. She left a curt message, stating she'd missed the plane and would be home tomorrow, late.

What was she going to do now? Where was she going to spend the night? A motel? Her heart skipped as a vision of herself—curled on a bed, pillow clutched to her chest, her eyes riveted to the door—flashed into her mind. No. Giving her statement to the police had dredged up every nightmarish aspect of her ordeal and now the memories lurked in the dark corners of her consciousness, taunting her.

She needed a friendly face, a sympathetic ear. Company. Craig Rival's face came easily to mind, and she recalled how gentle and concerned he'd been. She'd have given anything for some of that gentle concern tonight, but his attitude had changed when she couldn't produce the faux Purity.

Maybe Teri was home. She dug a tiny address book from her purse. The pages were water warped, the ink smeared, her old friend's name barely legible, her address and phone number blue blots. Thankfully, Teri Dean was listed in the local directory.

Teri sounded surprised but happy to hear Lyssa was at SeaTac, and before she could even ask, Teri insisted she stay overnight at her apartment in Kent.

"Great," Lyssa said. "Then I'll see you in about twenty minutes."

She hurried through the airport toward the multilevel parking garage. It was well-lighted, but as her footsteps echoed on the concrete floor, she felt vulnerable, exposed, half expecting a sinister figure in a raincoat and low-slung hat to leap from behind one of the vehicles and club her. She glanced around repeatedly, biting down the panic. At last, she spotted the Taurus she'd leased—no more small cars after her previous harrowing incident—and hastened inside, relocking the doors.

The creepy feeling stayed with her as Lyssa drove to Kent and into the Palms, one of a cluster of apartment complexes near River Bend Golf Complex, an eighteen-hole course spread out on the banks of the Green River. She found building C, a three-story, tan affair with forest green trim, and pulled forward into a visitor parking spot opposite. As she shut off the engine, she glanced in her rearview mirror and noticed Teri standing in one of the ground-floor doorways, waving goodbye to a man.

It looked like . . . Kevin?

Lyssa cranked her head around and stared out the car's rear window. The man wheeled away from Teri, and his face was revealed in the porch light. It *was* Kevin.

What was he doing at Teri's?

A memory stirred at Kevin's familiar stride. Long ago, she'd suspected him of coming on to Teri. Teri had denied it, but Lyssa had always wondered if her friend was sparing her feelings.

Kevin headed toward her car. Lyssa turned quickly in her seat, watching him once again in the mirror.

She had forgotten her suspicions after Teri met and married Mason Dean and moved to the Northwest, but situations had changed. Teri had been widowed for three years, she and Kevin divorced for two. They were both welcome to see whomever they pleased.

Near her trunk, Kevin stopped. He glanced at his watch, apparently reading it in the glow of the street lamp. His chestnut hair was stylishly tumbled, his face tanned, angular, perfect. Why hadn't she noticed the stinginess around his pale eyes until it was too late? A fleeting image of generous coffee-dark eyes teased her, and she brushed the thought of Craig Rival away as if it were a pesky fly.

Kevin gazed up and for half a second seemed to stare right at her. Lyssa's pulse jumped. Had he seen her sitting here? She steeled her resolve, then let out a huge sigh as he moved to the car beside hers. With her back to him, she pretended to fidget with something on the seat, silently screaming at him to drive away.

Finally, he did.

Sneaking a last glance at him in the side-view mirror, Lyssa felt a sudden shiver, as if she'd nearly stepped barefoot on a scorpion.

"HOW'D YOU GET IN HERE?"

Craig jerked around, his heart in his throat. The voice belonged to a stranger, a tall woman who was exactly the kind Uncle Wayne couldn't resist: long legs in a brown skirt the color of her eyes, ample bosom in a blouse as creamy as her skin, and flame hair tied back in a clip.

He ignored her question. "Where the hell is the Collection?"

"Wh-who are you?" She backed away a step, her hand snaking around the edge of the counter to the silent alarm.

"Don't touch that alarm." His temper and his patience snapped at the same time. "I'm Craig Rival."

Her hand went to her chest, and she gulped shallow breaths, as if he'd scared the daylights out of her, which he realized belatedly he most likely had. He wasn't exactly dressed for the office, and the bruise on his forehead gave him an angry appearance.

She was gazing at it with interest, a frown flickering in her eyes. "M-Mr. Rival," she stammered. "Please, accept my apology. We didn't expect you today. Stacey left for a few minutes. When the chime went off, I thought she'd returned. But... when I saw you..." Her eyes were again on the bruise. "Well, I suppose I thought you were..." She shrugged, apparently not wanting to call her new boss a burglar—at least, not to his face.

"Who are you?" Craig was sick and tired of women he didn't know showing up in unexpected places. He had a fleeting thought of Lyssa and it reminded him that the Collection, including the Purity, was missing from the display case. "Where is the Collection?"

"Why...in the vault. There have been a rash of burglaries in the area over the past three months and Way— Uh...Mr. Riv— The other Mr. Rival, your uncle, insisted the Collection not be left out for any reason."

Craig had started past her the second she'd said *vault*. He skirted the long counter in the middle of the room and ducked into the offices beyond.

The woman followed, chattering. "I'm Ginger Van Allen. Way— Your uncle hired me about a year ago as salesclerk. Stacey will verify that when she returns."

Craig had already figured out that she was an employee hired in his absence. He found the vault standing open and rushed inside. Ginger arrived on his heels. "Where?" he demanded.

She pointed to a corner. He pulled his loupe from his pocket and began lifting jewelry-box lids, doing a rapid inventory, his heartbeat leveling off with each piece accounted for, the jumping in his belly also abating. He felt suddenly exhausted. Yet joyous. It was all here, including the Russian czarina's tiara. Including the Purity. The genuine Purity.

His budding trust of Lyssa Carlyle shattered as if it were made of zircons, like the faux she'd claimed she'd made. He gnashed his teeth together. She had to have lied about it. She'd said it herself: there wasn't any way Wayne could have returned this necklace from Windance after suffering a fatal heart attack. But she'd seemed so honest.

Doubts swept him. Could someone else have discovered the necklace at Windance and returned it to the vault before Craig could find it missing? "Do you know Ginger whether or not my uncle ever had cause to remove the Purity from the premises?"

He could have sworn the question startled her. "N-no way. Mr. Rival would never do that."

Craig got the impression she was trying to convince them both. He gently replaced the Purity in its box. If Wayne had taken the Purity to Windance, he certainly wasn't the one who'd returned it to this vault. Who might have? Who else had had the opportunity? Stacey? David? They'd claimed Wayne's body at Belmont Hospital. Then why hadn't David mentioned it? Maybe he didn't know. Maybe Stacey had taken a tour of the house and found the necklace. Necklaces? Would she admit it if she had?

The chime sounded, and a moment later, the subject of his speculation appeared. "Cousin Craig. How wonderful! You look awful." Her hazel eyes lifted to the bruise. "But David assures me the concussion is mild?"

"Yes," he answered, studying her. Stacey Rival reminded Craig of a petite Morticia Addams. She had her father's slight build and pale Scandinavian coloring, but she dyed her straight, shoulder-length hair black and chose ghoulish lipsticks, which gave her face a pallid, exaggerated tone, as if she were a Halloween vampire. Her fingernails were painted black, he noticed, no doubt to match her clothing, which always tended toward mourning wear. "I was just asking Ginger if your dad might have had reason to take the Purity to Windance anytime over the past three months?"

He noticed a slight tensing of Stacey's jaw. Then she smiled, but her smile was chilly. "The only time Dad was at Windance was to check on the place . . . and the incompetent caretaker you left in charge. He certainly never took any jewelry with him on those occasions."

"Did David also tell you that a Lyssa Carlyle claims Wayne let her make a copy of the Purity?"

Stacey's eyes narrowed. "She's lying. You knew Dad better than that."

But the issue of how well he'd known Wayne kept cropping up, Craig mused as he climbed into the taxi an hour later and gave the address for his condo on Queen Anne Hill. It was preferable to think Lyssa Carlyle was the liar here, but a large part of her story seemed plausible. He shouldn't care. Not any longer. He had the Purity. The Collection was intact.

Rain washed the windows, obscuring his view of the town he'd called home for more than ten years. It was too dark to see anything much, anyway. He settled back in the seat as the cab rolled through traffic in starts and stops. Damn. He wanted the truth. All of it. It seemed the only way to make sense of the attack on Lyssa.

And then, as if night were suddenly morning and all that had been hidden in darkness was now revealed, he knew what had had him worried earlier that day. Why had whoever attacked Lyssa come back to Windance after making a clean escape from the police? Would someone who chose victims at random take such a risk? Fear wound tight around his heart. Where was Lyssa Carlyle?

TERI'S PERFECTLY ARCHED brown eyebrows shot upward as she opened the door and saw Lyssa standing in the porch light. "What in the world happened to you?"

Lyssa gave her a crooked grin, knowing her appearance had deteriorated to rag-mop status, while Teri looked great with her frosted brown hair cut ultrashort and brushed forward, feathering the edges of her oval face, enhancing her powder blue eyes and high cheekbones. The only flaw in an otherwise charming face was a thin mouth that seemed prematurely down turned, a legacy of early widowhood. "You might be sorry you asked."

"Never." Teri swept Lyssa inside and closed the door against the rain that had started falling in huge dollops. The apartment smelled of peach potpourri and fresh coffee. It was newly built, decorated in a Southwestern motif, the white leather love seat and chair draped in pastel Indian-blanket throws. Above the gas fireplace hung a collage of desert watercolors. Obviously Arizona was still dear to Teri. "You like?"

Lyssa did and told her so as she set her bag on the floor near the door and headed straight for the inviting chair.

"Coffee?"

"Yes."

Teri was back immediately and curled on the love seat, tucking her feet beneath her. "You have great timing. If you'd been here a few minutes sooner, you'd have run smack into Kevin."

"Really?" Whatever was going on between her ex and Teri didn't interest Lyssa, and she decided the best way to discourage Teri from divulging any details was not to ask about it. "I'll bet you love having a putting green practically on your doorstep."

Teri looked disappointed and ignored her question altogether. "Aren't you even a tad curious about Kevin...what agency he's with, that he was on the cover of *GQ* last year?"

Lyssa shook her head, weariness washing through her like the rain washing the windows. "Not even a smidgen."

Teri shrugged as if she didn't believe it, and said, "Well, it was strictly business. C.J. lent him some jewelry for a shoot at Ocean Shores. Kevin is leaving for Texas tomorrow and I'm returning the pieces to the firm." C.J. was C.J. Temple, Teri's boss, and the owner of Temple's Trinkets & Treasures, one of Lyssa's clients, one of Rival Gem's competitors.

Lyssa said, "I thought you wanted to know how I came to look like a hobo."

"Okay, I can take a hint."

Teri's grin vanished as Lyssa gave her a terse recap of the events of the past twenty-four hours. She interrupted with an occasional expletive, tearing up at the horror of Lyssa's flight, laughing in shock at the recounting of her encounter with Craig Rival.

"You actually got him arrested?"

Lyssa nodded, chagrined. "In his own home."

"He's a real stuffed shirt." Teri laughed. "I imagine he was furious."

Recalling Craig Rival's strong embrace and the gentle way he'd calmed her, Lyssa couldn't imagine anyone less of a stuffed shirt. "Actually, he was...kind."

Teri gave her a hug. "I'm just glad you're okay."

"Yeah, me too." Lyssa laughed halfheartedly, but she was damned glad to be alive and in one piece.

Teri freshened their coffee, then resettled on the love seat, her face thoughtful. "What were you doing at Hood Canal, anyway?"

Lyssa felt heat spiral into her cheeks. Maybe she didn't usually blush because she didn't usually lie. In fact, she was normally forthright to the point of indiscretion and had had to school herself against speaking without thinking on the subject of the faux Purity. But she'd purposely omitted mention of it from her story. After all, she'd promised Wayne she'd keep it secret, and promises were things she didn't give lightly. Not even to rats like Wayne Rival. However, she supposed it didn't matter now that he was dead, now that the faux was gone.

She told Teri about her deal with Wayne, expecting and receiving an amazed reaction. But something about the response was phony, as put-on as Lyssa's had been that year when she was eight and had found her Christmas present in her mother's closet and had to act surprised and delighted about the party dress she'd gotten instead of the Barbie doll she'd wanted. Had Teri somehow already known?

An unsettling feeling crept over Lyssa, like a black cloud creeping across the night sky, almost invisible. She swallowed too fast and felt her throat seize in protest. She trusted Teri. She did. But as they continued to discuss mutual friends and family, she wasn't as relaxed as she had been before she'd mentioned copying the Purity.

At length, Teri asked, "You planning to stick around for Wayne's funeral?"

Lyssa nodded. "If you have an extra black dress."

Saturday

THE DRESS WASN'T BLACK, but it was appropriate. Wearing makeup and her hair swept up in a French roll, Lyssa felt close to her old self, except for her toes, which were pinched in the borrowed pumps.

She slid onto the pew next to Teri, who was seated beside C.J. Temple. By all accounts, C.J. was in her late forties, but could pass for thirty-five. She wore her auburn hair chin length in a straight, flattering cut that focused attention on her blue eyes. Her soft pink mouth had a fullness that suggested collagen treatments, and her nails reminded Lyssa of claws, but her clothes were always understated, always the best quality. The odd thing about C.J. was that in all the years Lyssa had known her, she'd never seen the woman wear a single piece of jewelry.

The service, held in a quaint chapel in Seattle, was well attended. As the minister began to speak, Lyssa felt a shiver track her spine, a sensation of danger close at hand, and it struck her how easily someone could hide in a crowd. Trying not to draw attention to herself, she stole sideways glances at the people in the pews nearest her own, noting that she recognized or did business with many of them. But would she recognize her pursuer if he was present? Fear twisted in her belly as she acknowledged her answer: not even if he looked her squarely in the eye.

She fought against the sudden chill washing through her, and tried to concentrate on what the minister was saying, but as he rambled on, she was hit with another awful thought, the thought of a funeral that might come sooner than anticipated, a thought precipitated by her early-morning call to Saguaro County General. Grandy clung to life by a thread. A thread of hope? How she dreaded showing up without the Purity!

The graveside service was thankfully brief, and as the sun finally broke apart the cloud cover, the large gathering began to disperse. It was then that Lyssa finally caught more than a glimpse of Craig. He was flanked on one side by the man who'd driven them to Belmont yesterday—David something or other—and on the other by a slight woman with black hair and bloodred lips, who held his arm as if it were all that kept her standing.

Lyssa's heels sank into the rain-dampened earth as C.J., Teri and she inched forward, joining those moving toward the trio to offer condolences. Water crept up the sides of the ill-fitting pumps, soaking her pinched feet. "Who's that woman next to Craig Rival?" she whispered to Teri.

Teri craned her neck, then said, "Stacey. Wayne's daughter."

"His daughter?" Lyssa had a hard time digesting this. In all their hours together, Wayne hadn't once mentioned a daughter. Or anyone named Stacey. Odd that discovering she was Craig's cousin should evoke a speck of relief when pity would have been more appropriate. Judging from the way the woman was clinging to Craig, Lyssa supposed she must have loved her father as much as Lyssa loved hers. She'd need support, too, if she lost her dad—an unthinkable notion.

Car engines started, disturbing the solemn morning as the first few mourners began to leave.

Unexpectedly, Lyssa felt the skin at her neck prickle, again that sensation someone was watching her. On an indrawn breath, she glanced sharply around. Right, then left. No one seemed to be paying particular attention to her. She let out a taut sigh and shoved both hands into the pockets of her raincoat. She was probably being paranoid, understandable after what she'd been through, but it would likely be a good long time before she was again comfortable in crowds or alone.

It didn't help matters that she was worried how Craig Rival would react to her being here. Feigning interest in Teri's conversation with C.J., Lyssa strove to look everywhere but at Craig. It was an impossible task—she'd never been more aware of anyone. Repeatedly, no matter how hard she tried to resist, her gaze stole to him. Had he pushed that wayward lock of hair over the bruise in order to deter inquiries about it? Or had the gentle wind ruffled it? She'd bet it was the former. He didn't strike her as a man who tolerated whimsy.

Maybe he *was* a stuffed shirt.

Craig lifted his head, and as if by some inner radar, found her in the gathering. His expression skipped from surprise to curiosity, then to something unreadable, yet urgent. A tingle sped through her, sensuous, insidious and undeniable. For half a second, she fancied distant times and distant shores, maidens conquered by conquistadors. Her greeting smile slipped at the sudden lurch in her stomach.

No question about it. She was definitely physically attracted to this man. Of all the impossible situations.

Teri caught her arm. "Do you want to speak to Craig again, after yesterday?"

Lyssa knew she ought to run as far and as fast as she could. Perversely, she stood her ground. "Why not? I haven't done anything wrong. Besides, he's seen me now."

C.J. had already spoken to Craig and his cousin and was just moving away, hurrying after a prestigious Amsterdam diamond merchant, when a woman with flame red hair cut in front of Teri and Lyssa. There was something horribly familiar about the way she stood, something about her voice.

"Oh, no. Lyssa, I should have told you," Teri whispered, her eyes pinched with dread.

"Told me what?" Lyssa frowned at Teri.

The redhead glanced back at them. Her eyes rounded and her bottom lip dropped open as she spun to face Lyssa.

Lyssa's mouth went dry. What the hell was her cousin—the cousin she'd found in bed with her ex-husband—doing at Wayne Rival's funeral? "Ginger?"

Chapter Seven

"Well. Lyssa." Ginger Van Allen appeared to quickly recover her initial shock. Only an unnatural pink on her neck hinted that she might be feeling at all uncomfortable. "Whatever are you doing here?"

Lyssa held herself as stiff as one of the nearby headstones, too aware that Craig Rival was listening to this exchange, and she regretted she hadn't given in to her earlier instinct to run from this place and all its dangers. But she hadn't. And as awkward as this encounter was, she was adult enough to get through it. "I might ask you the same thing."

"Why, I work for Rival Gems International. Didn't Uncle Denny mention it?" Uncle Denny was Dennis Van Allen, Lyssa's father. Respecting her feelings, he rarely mentioned Ginger, except for the occasional lecture on what a shame it was that out of all they'd shared as children and teenagers and women, all the good and not so good moments, the only thing Lyssa associated with her cousin now was betrayal. He thought she ought to forgive Ginger. After all, they were family, and he knew firsthand the harm family discord could cause.

But Ginger didn't seem to need absolution from Lyssa. It was just as well, since Lyssa wasn't sure she could ever forgive the betrayal.

"Why didn't you tell her?" Ginger asked Teri.

Lyssa glanced at her friend and decided the oversight hadn't been intentional. She willed herself to relax. "I guess Dad and Teri knew I wouldn't be interested."

Ginger sighed. "Whatever." She brushed past Lyssa and moved toward the flower-draped casket, nibbling at her pinkie fingernail, something she only did when she was upset. Also, Lyssa realized belatedly, her eyes were underscored by those dark blue splotches she always got whenever she'd spent any length of time crying. Maybe she could have been kinder.

Teri was grimacing, conveying an apology with the pressure of her grasp on Lyssa's arm. Thankfully, she too seemed aware that they were being scrutinized by Craig and Stacey.

"Ms. Dean and Ms. Carlyle, an unexpected twosome," Craig said, gazing at Lyssa as if he couldn't believe the sophisticated woman she'd been transformed into had any connection with the grungy, terrorized ragamuffin he'd spent hours with the day before. She read approval in his dark eyes and something inherently more dangerous: interest. "Thank you for coming. Lyssa, have you met Stacey, Wayne's daughter?"

From a distance, she hadn't thought Stacey resembled her late father, but now Lyssa could see that she did, especially her hazel eyes. Her attire, however, was unique. She wore black like a coat of fur, and whenever she moved, the excess of bracelets on both wrists jangled. Lyssa couldn't help thinking of a belled cat.

"Nice to meet you." Lyssa reached to shake Stacey's hand, but Stacey only glared at her. Feeling foolish, and somewhat puzzled, Lyssa drew back her hand and stuffed it into her coat pocket. Apparently Craig had told this woman about the faux, and she, also, was of the opinion that Lyssa was a liar out to defame the good name of Wayne Rival. She shouldn't have expected anything more. Not from any of the Rivals. She shouldn't have come to this service. "I'm sorry about your father," she said, then beat a quick retreat in the general direction of Teri's car.

She *was* sorry about Wayne. On the one hand. On the other hand, if he hadn't stolen her faux wedding necklace, she wouldn't have almost been murdered. Lyssa stifled an urge to shudder as an unpleasant thought popped into her head. What if the attack on her was somehow connected to neither necklace being at Windance? Was that as farfetched as it seemed? Suddenly she wanted to leave. She glanced around for Teri, but Teri had been waylaid by one of the few people in attendance today that Lyssa didn't recognize. She hesitated.

A familiar jangle sounded behind her, and a second later David and Stacey brushed by her, heading for the waiting limousine. Over his shoulder, David called, "Are you coming, Craig?"

"In a moment."

He was right behind her. Lyssa tensed. Over her shoulder, he said, "I thought you'd be in Arizona by now."

She drew a slow breath, trying to still the dizzying tingle sweeping through her at the sound of his voice. Somehow, she managed to face him without her knees giving way. "Couldn't get a flight until early tonight."

There was an odd glint of longing in his eyes that spoke to the desire swirling inside her, but he sounded all business when he asked, "Have you known Teri Dean long?"

"We've been friends since junior high school. If you're wondering whether or not she'll give me a character reference, I'm sure she would—an exemplary one." They both knew he wasn't asking for references. No, it was more likely that he was interested in how long and what kind of business she might have with his biggest competitor, C.J. Temple. Or perhaps he just wanted to know where the alleged faux Purity fit into the mix.

Well, she'd told him the truth, and she was getting weary of not being believed. Granted, she had no proof, but that was his problem. She knew she was honest. Lyssa tilted her head. "How long have you known my cousin Ginger?"

That got his eyebrows lifting. "Ginger Van Allen is related to the DeHavilands?"

She ought to let him squirm, but she supposed she'd done more than enough damage to him already. "Not really. She's related on my father's side of the family."

He glanced over at the limo, obviously anxious to leave. "You know, I'd really like to believe your story, but the Purity was at my office in Seattle when I got there last night—in the vault, where Ginger and Stacey claim it's been for the past three months."

Now Lyssa's eyebrows lifted, then squashed in a frown. Craig could believe the Purity had been in Seattle the past three months if he wanted, but she knew otherwise. And obviously he hadn't found the faux with it or he'd have said as much. The shudder she'd stifled before raced through her. Had her wild thought any substance? Had someone tried to kill her because of the two necklaces?

It seemed crazy. And yet, whoever had closed Windance after Wayne's death must have removed both necklaces. But who? She stole a glance at the limo. Stacey? If Wayne had told his daughter about the copy, she might have taken the necklaces to keep Craig from finding out what her father had been up to. She had access to the Rival vault in Seattle, so returning the Purity would have been no problem for her. Lyssa felt an anxious twinge. What had become of the faux? Had it been destroyed? The thought made her heartsick.

But even worse was imagining Craig's cousin trying to kill her. What possible reason could she have—could anyone have? Craig would never accept such a thing, and Lyssa didn't even bother suggesting it. "I guess you're going to believe whatever you want or need to believe, but I think you're trusting someone you shouldn't."

Craig's expression went thoughtful. Yet, reading indecision in his hesitation, she sensed he wanted to believe her. As if to confirm it, he said, "If you had one shred of evidence that the faux purity even exists..."

The frustration she'd reined in like a frisky colt popped a restraint, threatening to break free and trample anything and everything in its path. It jarred loose something she should have remembered before now, and she smiled at Craig. "I haven't any proof the necklace exists, but I do have proof of intent. Wayne insisted on a legal agreement between us. I can fax you a copy of it."

Craig looked skeptical, as if he, too, thought she should have mentioned this sooner. "What kind of an agreement?"

He'd stepped impossibly closer, and she seemed unable to draw a full breath. Somehow she managed to say, "Skipping all the legal terminology, it allows me to make the copy for my personal enjoyment, but restricts me from ever selling it for personal gain."

"Who drew up the agreement?"

She tried to recall, then suddenly it came—and with it the last name of his lawyer friend David: Lundeen, Lundeen and Lundeen, the law firm on the papers tucked in her vault. Was Craig's friend in on the theft with Stacey? She nodded toward the limousine. "Why don't you ask David?"

The muscle in his jaw tensed as he stared at her with fire burning in his dark eyes. Either he wanted to tell her to go to hell, or he wanted to kiss her. Lyssa glanced away, an unsteadiness wobbling through her.

"David's already told me that Wayne never mentioned you." Craig's voice was husky. "He wouldn't lie to me."

His hot breath fanned her cheeks, her eyelashes. Lyssa's gaze locked with his, her heart thrumming like a lightly strummed violin, and she said in a breathy whisper, "I didn't ask Wayne who drew up the agreement." She swallowed and continued in a firmer tone. "Maybe it wasn't David. There's more than one Lundeen on the firm's letterhead and, as I recall, the signature is a messy scrawl. I suppose you can figure that out when I send you the fax."

Instead of answering, Craig grabbed hold of her upper arms and pulled her against him, kissing her hard and full on the mouth like a man long deprived of loving. Surprise and desire collided inside Lyssa, hot emotion hitting cold resistance and steaming all agitation from her.

Craig seemed suddenly to realize where they were. He pulled back, jerkily releasing her. Confusion and desire struggled for control of his features.

Lyssa caught sight of Teri nearing at the same moment that a horn blast erupted from the limousine.

Craig looked as if he wanted to explain. But all he said was, "Don't forget the fax."

Lyssa's face burned, but she couldn't ascertain whether she was embarrassed or disappointed. "I'll send it right after I see Grandy."

"Good. Well—" He paused, then smirked, touching his bruised forehead gingerly. " 'It's been nice to know you' doesn't seem appropriate... but I don't suppose I'll ever forget you."

Unwittingly, Lyssa brushed her fingertips across her mouth. "Nor I, you."

A moment later, he was gone.

Lyssa stared after the departing limousine, feeling dismissed and strangely empty, wondering why he'd kissed her.

CRAIG COULDN'T STOP wondering why he'd kissed Lyssa. He did nothing impulsively. It went against his nature. And yet, he just had. Why? He wanted to end the relationship with her. Didn't he? Then why couldn't he quit thinking about her? Her problems were not his concern, just as today was not the day to question David—or the other Lundeens—about Wayne and her.

Still, he couldn't shake the questions from his mind. Maybe it was the earnest glint in those sea green eyes of hers. Maybe it was his worry that the attack on her wasn't random. Or maybe the truth lived in his unexpected and disconcerting attraction to her. The passion underlying their kiss.

Craig tried mingling, but it wasn't long before he realized his wool-gathering was perturbing some of the postfuneral guests at Stacey's. And the cobwebs crisscrossing his mind kept thickening. He wanted answers, and the thought of waiting another twenty-four hours at best before the fax arrived had him on edge. A Scotch on the rocks only brought the beginnings of another headache. Deciding he had one course of action open to him, he left Stacey's as soon as propriety allowed.

It was midafternoon when he reached the office. He attacked Wayne's records expectantly, but an hour of digging through every paper and file he could lay his hands on produced not a damned thing that pertained to Lyssa Carlyle or the DeHavilands. Enough was enough. He was dead on his feet.

The promise of a sunny afternoon was dying on a ridge of high clouds by the time he got into his Lexus. He drove to his condo, immune to the traffic and the familiar sights he'd longed to see only the night before, arguing with himself to bury all thought of Lyssa and the faux Purity as finally as he'd buried Uncle Wayne.

But she wouldn't be banished.

He dropped into his bed and shut his eyes, and there she was. The taste of her lips, the feel of her body against his haunted him. The woman had to be a witch. He could find no other explanation for the spell she'd cast over him. For it had to be a spell. Why else would he want her so? Why else would he have kissed her—totally inappropriately—at his uncle's funeral?

Craig groaned and rolled onto his side, shoving deeper into the pillow. She was the most dangerous kind of woman, as innocent as a waif one moment, as seductive as a temptress the next. Thinking himself fortunate to have escaped with just a bump on the noggin and one not-too-innocent kiss, he drifted into sleep and dreamed of angels with golden hair and sea green eyes and diamond necklaces and omnipresent menace.

The phone beside his bed startled him awake. Dusk filled the room, but the luminous dial of the clock said it was still afternoon, and now he heard the rain. He lifted the receiver. "Craig Rival."

There was a hesitation, then a woman said, "This is Roxanne DeHaviland, Mr. Rival. I'm trying to locate my daughter, Lyssa Carlyle... on a matter of extreme urgency."

Craig shoved to a sitting position, frowning. How had Lyssa's mother gotten his private phone number? He was about to ask, when he remembered the telephone at Windance had call forwarding, and the woman had said it was a matter of extreme urgency. "Is her grandmother worse?"

Again she hesitated, and Craig realized the impertinence of his question. It was none of his business. But before he could apologize, she said, "Yes. I'm afraid Lyssa will be too late with the Purity. The doctor doesn't expect Mother to live through the night."

The doctor doesn't expect mother to live through the night. He had more than a nodding acquaintance with that phrase. It brought a shiver to his warm skin—that and the tears he could hear in Roxanne DeHaviland's voice. His heart bled for her. He'd been there. Oh, yes, he had been there. "I'm sorry." The two most inadequate words in the English language at a time like this.

He told her to try Teri Dean and that he knew Lyssa couldn't get a flight home until the evening. But he hadn't the stomach to tell her there would be no Purity to comfort the dying woman.

He showered, shaved and dressed in fresh black jeans and black polo shirt, but didn't feel better. The anguish in Roxanne's voice had aroused unpleasant memories of his mother's illness. Craig wished there was some way he could help.

HAD SHE EVER FELT MORE helpless? Lyssa wondered, sinking onto a window seat near the wing of the plane. No. Not even with a maniac chasing her. Even then, she'd had courses of action and the hope that she'd somehow survive. But there was no course of action, no hope that Grandy would somehow survive. Nothing Lyssa could do would change that fact, nothing she could do would ease her grandmother's last hours.

Her fate was in God's hands, and it seemed He was calling His angel home.

With the back of her hand, Lyssa swiped at the tears welling in her eyes, bit down the lump in her throat and fastened her seat belt. She'd been among the first to board, but although the engines were gearing up, the seats next to hers remained vacant. As far as she was concerned, they could stay that way. She'd had her fill of strangers.

Her fill of Rivals, too.

She couldn't get out of Seattle soon enough, and didn't care to return. Her gaze drifted to the window, but all she saw was her own reflection. She yanked down the shade. Seattle wasn't to blame. Except for this weekend, the Emerald City had been good to her, launched her career—

Oh, blast it! Next weekend. She'd forgotten all about the Western Women-Owned Business Association's conference at the Four Seasons. Months ago, she'd promised to present a workshop.

Grandy...

Leaving now meant canceling on the conference coordinator at the last minute. Lyssa winced. Professional and personal reliability were important to her— as was her reputation, contrary to what Craig Rival thought of her. She blew out an annoyed breath. Why should she even care what that disturbing man thought of her? She shouldn't. Wouldn't. But the memory of his kiss lingered like the delicious aftertaste of a dinner mint. Why had he done it? Impulse? Was he curious to see how she'd respond? A goodbye?

This last thought panged her already aching heart, and she forced Craig Rival from her mind. Shutting out the purr of voices moving through the cabin as well, she rested her head against the seat, closed her eyes and thought instead of the woman she loved so dearly who was soon to be taken from her.

Idella DeHaviland—proud, principled, a true romantic—was the crown jewel in the DeHaviland family, and with all her heart she believed that not owning the wedding necklace, the Purity, was the only obstacle keeping her daughter Roxanne and her granddaughter Lyssa from finding true love. She prayed for one thing before she died: the return of the necklace to her family.

And somehow, she'd gotten it into her head that this miracle was going to happen.

Every day she'd become more certain of it, and every day Lyssa had known she would be disappointed, until finally Lyssa could bear it no longer. She'd contacted Wayne Rival and struck the deal. Her heart felt heavy. After all she'd done to make the miracle a reality, there was no Purity for Grandy.

Once again Craig Rival intruded on her thoughts. She could see his handsome face, his mocking manner as he questioned anew her motive in making the faux. Lyssa stretched her neck, working the kinks loose. What if he was right about Grandy knowing the real Purity when she saw it, when she held it? The copy was good. Not as blue as the Purity, though, and Grandy was intuitive. Would she guess?

RISING FROM AN AISLE SEAT three rows back, a figure strode toward Lyssa. Watching her. Hating her. *This woman has the power to destroy my life—if she remembers seeing me at Windance minutes before Wayne Rival's death.* Fear darted through the disguised killer. Had she already remembered? Already started wondering about it?

Already mentioned it to someone else?

A cold sweat broke across overheated flesh. *I can't risk letting her live much longer.* The killer took a step toward Lyssa's seat. The plane vibrated and overhead compartments banged as passengers stowed bags.

Two rows behind Lyssa.

A woman swung her arm into the aisle. The killer stopped and, bridling with anger, waited until the woman handed a coloring book to a child.

One row behind Lyssa.

Tunnel vision. The killer's gaze zeroed in on the back of her head, the hunter taking aim. She wouldn't get away this time. Her luck had run out.

A man stepped from the first-class section of the plane. The killer's attention twitched from Lyssa.

Not him. Not again. The killer blanched, barely biting back a growl of fury. Panic ran rampant through terror-frozen limbs. *Wait a minute. What am I so frightened of? My own mother wouldn't recognize me in this gray beard and scruffy wig, in these tinted glasses, these sloppy, old-man clothes, standing stooped as if by age.*

I'm completely safe.

Lyssa Carlyle was not.

Behind the killer, a flight attendant said, "Please take your seat, sir."

The killer smiled, confident the disguise was working.

SOMEONE SAT IN THE SEAT next to Lyssa. Reflexively, she twisted her hands together in her lap. She kept her eyes closed, suddenly afraid to open them, afraid to look at the stranger beside her, lest she see the face of her pursuer—and not even know it.

Chapter Eight

Lyssa kept her eyes closed, irrepressible fear gripping her as tightly as she gripped the arms of her seat. The plane lurched, began to roll, then its motion smoothed, and the engine's roar increased. She felt the lift and leveling off. Only then did she relax, drawing in a whiff of spicy cologne.

She heard a muted clank, like charms on a bracelet bumping together. A voice she recognized said, "You can take your seat belt off now."

Lyssa's heart stumbled and her eyelids flew open. Craig Rival was grinning devastatingly at her, an aura of innocence about him, as if it were the most natural thing in the world that he should be seated next to her on this flight to Phoenix. Every nerve in her body not already tensed by sheer imagination, tweaked. "You—?"

Craig winced at her tone and raised his right arm as if to ward off a blow. "You aren't going to hit me again, are you?"

A scowl pulled her brows together, but not one plausible explanation for his being on this plane would lift itself from the worry-exhausted mire of her brain. "Do I have reason to hit you?"

He shrugged and leaned closer.

"Can't think of any reason." His warm breath caressed her face and Lyssa wondered if he was going to kiss her again—*wanted* him to kiss her again.

She pulled back, disconcerted by his nearness and the memory of his mouth on hers. She was too tired to play games, and far too susceptible to the low heat of desire that his voice stirred inside her. "What are you doing here?"

"Here, you mean?" He pointed to his seat. "Oh, that was easy. I traded my first-class ticket with the guy who had this seat."

He noticed she was wearing the ragged jeans and red sweater she'd worn at Windance yesterday, but her hair was still upswept as it had been this afternoon, loose strands feathering her face. His muscles tightened as he remembered their kiss, as he responded to this new look that had little in common with the waif or the temptress; indeed it was more alluring, more touchable, the most dangerous yet. She folded her arms across her chest as if to guard her heart against the attraction that pulled them together, but he knew that wouldn't protect either of them. He wanted to kiss her again.

Lyssa could see that he wanted to kiss her again. Ignoring the delicious tremor racing through her, she noticed he was wearing all black—shirt, jeans, a leather jacket slung across his lap—like some character in a second-rate gangster movie. But there was nothing second-rate about Craig Rival, nothing sinister and, at the moment, nothing safe. She eyed him skeptically. "I suppose you have business in Arizona?"

His business in Arizona was personal. Some of it, he would tell her. Some of it, he would not. "As a matter of fact..."

"Sure you do, and it was so pressing you had to take *this* plane. What's really going on, Mr. Rival?" The creepy feeling she'd had before she'd opened her eyes returned in a rush, chasing away all sensuous thoughts and feelings and drawing shivers on her warm flesh.

"I thought we'd settled all that first-name stuff."

Why was he deliberately sidestepping her questions? Deliberately making her uneasy? She'd pegged him earlier as a man who did nothing on the spur of the moment, and here he was, disproving that theory. But why? She'd promised to fax the agreement. And he'd seemed glad, delighted even, that she'd be out of his life. Her patience snapped. "If you'd rather not tell me what moved you to catch this flight...Craig, please forget I asked."

Satisfaction curled in her stomach as his brows lifted and surprise crossed his face. She released her seat belt and shifted away from him, snapped up the shade and stared out the window as if she could see something besides her own reflection.

Pressing his head back against the seat, Craig blew out a long, slow breath. At length, he said in a quiet voice, "I take it your mother reached you?"

Lyssa jerked around and studied his gentle expression. Not for the first time, she decided his bold face hid a compassionate soul, but his mention of her mother's telephone call renewed the anxious churning in her stomach. "Yes."

"She told me your grandmother was critical." Empathy shone in his dark eyes.

A lump clogged Lyssa's throat. "It doesn't sound good."

The gravity of the situation hung between them.

Craig said, "I found myself wanting to help—"

"About all anyone can do now is pray."

"That's what I thought. At first. Then it occurred to me that I had the power to do something no one else could."

Lyssa frowned as he swept his jacket off his lap, revealing a black leather briefcase. Again she heard that charm-bracelet tinkle. Now she saw the source: a chain linked Craig's left wrist to his briefcase. Apparently he was carrying something of value. He stared down at the case as if looking at her made him uncomfortable.

"It seemed a tragedy that Idella DeHaviland not hold the Purity a last time."

Lyssa's eyes widened. Had she heard him right? Had he caught this plane in order to grant the dying wish of a woman he'd never even met? Hope stirred, stealing her breath. His gaze was on her now, sinking every conceivable reason she'd raised for resisting her attraction to him. She placed her hand on the lid of the briefcase. "The Purity?"

He nodded.

She could have sworn an electrical current zinged the palm resting on the sleek, black leather. Grandy's miracle was actually happening—in part, at least. The Purity wasn't being returned to the DeHavilands permanently, but perhaps letting Grandy think that would ease her last moments. Tears pooled in Lyssa's eyes and her heart thumped. "Why?"

A trace of heat inched up Craig's neck. He wasn't doing this for the thanks; he preferred his grand gestures went uncredited, and without his personal participation. The truth of the matter was, Roxanne DeHaviland had touched him where he lived, but how could he say that to her daughter without sounding like a sentimental sap? He couldn't. "The situation with your grandmother…reminded me of my mother. I knew she'd want me to do this."

Lyssa shook her head, still reeling from the fact that this thing might actually happen—if Grandy held on awhile longer. Her mother would say she was naive trusting another Rival, but her own instincts told her that Craig expected nothing in return. She couldn't remember the last time anyone or anything had touched her this much. Lyssa beamed at him. "I don't know what to say—except thank you."

Craig tried to look away, chagrined at the wonder and adulation in those gorgeous eyes of hers. A worm of guilt wriggled through the good feeling filling him. He hadn't caught this plane simply to bring the Purity to Idella DeHaviland's bedside. No sir. The primary reason was to extricate Lyssa Carlyle from his system—no matter what it took.

He switched subjects. "I had the distinct impression you were trying to tell me something about my cousin Stacey this afternoon. What?"

Lyssa had wanted to forget about the attack on her, at least for a while longer. She sighed. "I know that the Purity was at Windance last Monday night. But you found it in Seattle, in your office vault. We've agreed that Wayne didn't have time to return it there, but it seems logical that Stacey might have had not only opportunity when she came down to identify and claim her father's body, but also motive, in that she might not want you to know what Wayne had been doing."

He, too, had considered this. He nodded, then raised his eyebrows. "That means you suspect Stacey has your faux and that she is lying about it all?"

"More than that. It occurred to me that she might have been the one who attacked me."

Her comment provoked a startled laugh from Craig. "Stacey? I thought the police were looking for a man."

"Are they? I told them I couldn't tell whether a man or woman was driving the Cadillac. The person was of average height and build, and I never saw a face nor heard a voice."

"Still . . . Stacey?" He was smirking. "I can't picture it, but let's say you're right. What reason would she have for wanting you dead?"

Lyssa sighed. She'd known he wouldn't believe anything negative about his cousin. "To shut me up about the faux Purity, probably."

"Why?" He obviously didn't believe this, either.

She couldn't blame him. It sounded absurd. She sighed again. Too many important pieces of this puzzle were missing. "I don't know. But somehow I'm sure it has to do with the faux wedding necklace."

WAYNE RIVAL'S SLAYER glared at the back of Lyssa's head, swearing silently, hating her more with every breath, fearing her worse, wishing her dead. What in blazes was Craig Rival doing on this plane? A mere two nights ago that woman had knocked him cuckoo and trussed him up like a Christmas goose in the kitchen at Windance. Now they acted like old chums.

A frown puckered the killer's mouth, tugging the glued beard painfully. What was she saying to Craig with their heads bent so close together? Icy fear spread through every artery. What in hell had she told him? Was she telling him now?

With trembling fingers, the killer hoisted the plastic glass of whiskey the flight attendant had provided and downed half of it, then mopped at the spillage on the false beard with a cocktail napkin. Stupid nuisance disguise. The liquor burned going down, but soon was soothing ragged nerves, and reviving confidence. Stay calm. Sure, this was risky, but the rewards would be many—like the rush that killing Wayne had given.

The killer took another swallow of whiskey, striving to drown or dull the worries that still niggled. *I have to find out what they're up to. Craig Rival might also need eliminating.*

But first I'll take care of her.

The killer gazed toward Lyssa again and smiled a nasty little grin, fingering the empty hypodermic in one pocket. One quick prick. A little air in her veins. That was all it required, and it would look like she'd died of a heart attack. This was going to be the rush of all rushes. No more reprieves. *I just need a couple seconds alone with her.*

Saguaro County General, an aged adobe structure, sat on the edge of the desert. Night pressed down on them, offering little in the way of scenery, but Craig was certain that black lump in the distance was Camelback Mountain. Palm and orange trees and saguaro cacti dotted the parking lot. Few cars occupied visitor spaces this time of night. Lyssa parked her car and led him, through the chilly evening that smelled of impending rain, to the front entrance.

Lyssa's nerves were skittish as she and Craig strode through the deserted lobby, making for the bank of elevators. His boot heels clumped against the polished linoleum and the drone of a vacuum seemed to say, *Hurry, hurry.* Would they be in time? Would Grandy actually be able to hold the Purity? Hope buoyed Lyssa onto the elevator and she stepped to the rear, instructing Craig to push the fourth-floor button. The light glowed red like a stop signal holding up their progress. "Maybe we should take the stairs," he suggested.

"No. It's just annoyingly slow." The elevator was as old as the hospital, smelling of disinfectants and other seamier smells she'd didn't want identified.

When she thought her lungs would explode from impatience, the door finally began closing. An elderly man with a youthful gait rushed forward and scrambled aboard. He smelled as if he'd bathed in whiskey, but he didn't seem drunk. Obviously a street person. Her heart went out to him, and she wondered what he was doing in the hospital this late. Seeking a warm place to spend the night?

Struggling to keep from wrinkling her nose, Lyssa averted her eyes and stared at her scuffed sneakers. Then at Craig's feet. Cowboy boots—lizard or snakeskin as near as she could judge. In need of polishing.

But the old man had on a new pair of Nikes. Expensive Nikes. Odd. The rest of his clothing was old and battered, something a mugger might wear.

A mugger! She froze. Had he noticed the briefcase clamped to Craig's wrist and followed them?

The old man's face was indistinguishable beneath a bushy beard, his eyes hidden by his hat and glasses with opaque lenses. But he seemed to be staring intently at the briefcase. Was he going to pull a gun and rob them? A shiver tracked her spine. She grasped Craig's left elbow, pulling herself against his side, pressing the briefcase containing the Purity between them. Craig lifted his eyebrows slightly, but there was pleased surprise in his eyes. He folded his hand over her much smaller one, sending shock waves up her arm, along with a sense of security that she somewhat resented but desperately needed. "We're almost there."

"I know. I'm just afraid—"

"Hush. Don't even think that."

She tried rolling her eyes, in hopes that Craig would understand it was the other passenger in the elevator who had her frightened. The old man was snuffling now, as if from a sinus condition. Lyssa held stiffly to Craig, half expecting a gun barrel to jam her ribs at any second.

The ride ended. To Lyssa's relief, the man stayed aboard as they disembarked and headed for the cancer ward.

A woman slouched on a chair in the waiting room, exhaustion written in the hollows of her thin face. Her long straight hair might once have been as sun bright as Lyssa's, but was now a flat brass with silver streaks running through it. Spotting them, she instantly came to life, bolting to her feet, a smile of welcome aimed directly at Lyssa.

Lyssa smiled back, noting the slight twitch of her mother's brows as she noticed Craig. She hadn't told Roxanne anything about her ordeal. It would only have upset her, and she had worry enough on her mind with Grandy. But her questions couldn't be put off forever, and there would be plenty when she introduced Craig Rival. None of them easy to answer. Her mother and her grandmother had nothing good to say about the Rival family.

"Darlin' mine, you're a sight for sore eyes."

Lyssa sighed, falling into Roxanne's outstretched arms, savoring the comfort and the scent of perfume that always clung to her mother.

Craig stood to one side, watching the welcome with a twinge of envy. Roxanne was inches taller than Lyssa and she peered at him with curiosity in her blue eyes. Then she held Lyssa away from her and said, "Here now. Wipe off those tears. She's still hanging on, but it won't do for her to see you're this upset."

Lyssa nodded. She'd managed to box her emotions inside and deal with getting through what she'd had to, but one hug from her mother and the package started bursting at the seams. She nodded and stepped back.

Glancing uncomfortably at Craig, Roxanne murmured, "Do you have it?"

There was no need to ask what. Lyssa drew a breath. "Craig, I'd like you to meet my mother, Roxanne DeHaviland. Mother, this is Craig Rival."

"Rival?" she choked. Her round eyes widened as if she'd just been introduced to a man from outer space—or worse, a mass murderer.

"He's brought the Purity for Grandy. The real one."

"What happened to the faux?"

"It's a long story."

"That's all you've said since Friday. I guess we're going to have to find time for that lengthy tale of yours. Right now, however..." She eyed Craig with potent puzzlement. "Did she say you'd brought the Purity for my mother? Are you finally going to sell it back to us?"

There was no mistaking the hostility in her tone; she didn't think the Rivals had any right to the Purity. He knew of the DeHavilands' attempts to purchase the necklace over the past twenty years, but they didn't seem to appreciate that the necklace meant as much to his family as it did to their own. "Well, no, actually—"

Lyssa jumped in. "Really, Mom. It was beyond the call of duty for Craig to bring this. Doesn't Grandy always say not to look a gift horse in the mouth?"

Roxanne sputtered, glancing from one to the other, obviously not satisfied with either of their answers. "Has the world gone stark-raving mad, or only me?"

"Can we see Grandy?"

Lyssa knew from her expression that Roxanne wasn't going to let this drop, but she was striving to be as civil as her upbringing demanded and as her ragged nerves allowed. For that, Lyssa was grateful.

Roxanne led them into the ward. "She comes in and out of consciousness. There's been a slight improvement since we spoke this afternoon."

The nurse cautioned them against tiring her patient, then allotted them five minutes alone with her. The room smelled medicinal, acidic, and Lyssa winced at all that they'd been putting Grandy through. She was lying on the bed like a grand racehorse, brought to its knees but not beaten. Her eyes opened slowly like flowers budding to reveal petals the bright blue of the ocean. Her skin was as delicate as aged lace, with a tinge of unnatural grayness. Her head was wrapped in a turban, her thick snowy hair lost to chemotherapy.

"Lyssa?" Her voice lacked its former timbre. She struggled to raise her head, a look of expectancy on her shrunken face.

Lyssa hurried forward and straightened the turban, knowing how particular her grandmother was about appearances, especially when men were in the vicinity. She kissed her on the cheek and took hold of her hand. "Please, Grandy, don't strain yourself. I'm not going anywhere."

Hopeful blue eyes studied her. "I've been waiting for you."

Behind her, Lyssa could hear Craig clicking the locks of the briefcase. A second later, he was at the bedside, holding a length of velvet in his palms. She didn't even introduce him. "Grandy, we've brought you something."

Craig lowered the velvet to her lap, then slowly folded back the edges of cloth. As the blue light of the Purity was revealed, so was a sparkle in those ocean blue eyes.

"Oh, my. Oh, my." Grandy's voice was weak, but so full of emotion that Lyssa feared it was too much for her. "At long last. Thank you, God, thank you. And you, too, young man." She caught his hand. "Thank you. I don't know how you got it away from those nasty Rivals and I don't care. The Purity is finally back where it belongs."

Craig blanched. Idella wrapped her hands around the necklace and hugged it to her as if it were a long-lost child. Her eyes closed and she seemed to drift off.

The nurse stepped in. "Time's up."

"The necklace," Craig whispered to Lyssa.

She reached for it, but Grandy held it tightly. Lyssa couldn't disentangle it from her. She glanced at Craig. "Uh . . . she's really clinging to it. Look, we'll be right outside. What harm can it do if she holds it awhile longer? No one is going to steal it from her."

He didn't like it, but he seemed to have no choice. "Okay."

"I'll let you know as soon as she awakens." The nurse shooed them from the room.

The waiting seemed interminable. Lyssa was dead on her feet, longing for her own bed and her own bath and a change of clothes. But she had Roxanne and Craig to deal with before she'd get any rest.

At least Roxanne was no longer looking at Craig like he was a pariah, someone she was only tolerating for the sake of others. Rather, she was studying him as if he were an enigma, as if she couldn't believe someone she despised so much could possess even a shred of decency. Lyssa wasn't sure what to think, but she could see Craig disliked the scrutiny.

He grinned, an ill-at-ease lifting of the corners of his mouth, and backed away from them as he spoke, clearly planning a getaway. "I don't know about you ladies, but I could use a cup of coffee. There must be a machine around here somewhere."

"Mr. Rival." Roxanne's voice was soft, but it stopped Craig. "I don't know what to think about all this, but please allow me to express my gratitude to you. I really never thought I'd lay eyes on the genuine Purity again. Although I had heard about it since I was born, I've only actually seen it once.

"Several years ago, Denny—Lyssa's father—and I visited your father's offices in Seattle. It was the first time I'd seen my great-grandmother's necklace in person. It was in some kind of display case Paul Rival called his Collection. We tried to purchase the Purity that day, but he wouldn't hear of it. In fact, he threatened to call security if we didn't leave."

Craig lifted an eyebrow. He had known about the DeHavilands' attempts over the years to buy back the Purity, but his father had never told him that they'd visited the Seattle office. "I apologize if my father was rude—"

"Rude?" Roxanne interrupted, the redness in her face a signal that *rude* was too polite a word for the way his father had treated them.

Lyssa feared her mother was about to launch into a tirade on that very topic, having been regaled with the recounting more times than she could recall. Both of her parents were emotionally charged and easily provoked, as proven by the constant verbal battles that had peppered their married life. She'd always suspected they rather enjoyed the arguing, but she had hated it. And she could only imagine the scene they'd made at the offices of Rival Gems International. She didn't want a repeat of it here and now.

"Mom..."

Roxanne nodded, then inhaled deeply and closed her eyes, obviously reining in the old anger. Eventually she said, "You can see what the Purity means to my mother, what it would mean to have the necklace once again in our family...where it belongs. Please tell me you'll allow us to purchase it."

Craig was starting to regret his impulse to make this trip with the Purity. First Idella DeHaviland defamed his family, then latched onto the necklace and wouldn't let go. And now Roxanne was playing on his sympathies to get him to sell the necklace to her. He really did need some coffee...laced with something stiff. "I'm sorry to disappoint you. The Purity means as much to me as it does to you. I have no intention of parting with it permanently, but after all that Lyssa had been through trying to recover the faux, I—"

Roxanne didn't wait for him to finish. She swung immediately to Lyssa. Motherly concern was etched in the worry lines around her eyes and mouth. "All that you've been through? Darlin' mine, I think we'd better hear that lengthy tale of yours, pronto."

Lyssa rolled her eyes. She was too tired for this, but that wouldn't dissuade her mother from insisting on every detail. She pointed to the bench outside Grandy's room. "Then let's sit down."

Craig excused himself, promising to return with coffee. Lyssa knew she was going to need it.

CRAIG BROUGHT THE WOMEN coffee, then excused himself again and returned to the machine he'd found near the cafeteria to get himself a cup. Figuring he'd give them another ten minutes, he leaned against the wall next to the coffee machine and slowly sipped the steaming liquid, surprised that it wasn't half-bad. But, he reflected, probably the last thing he needed was a jolt of caffeine. As it was, he was running on too few hours of sleep and too little food.

All because of Lyssa Carlyle.

He shoved his hand through his hair and glanced down the hall, catching sight of a door swinging open. A man appeared. The vagrant from the elevator. He stiffened visibly as if seeing Craig had startled him, then he retreated through the doorway and closed the door. The stairs, Craig realized. The guy must be sleeping in the stairwell. But then, why had he come into the hall and taken a chance of being seen?

Maybe he should report him to hospital security. But maybe the poor guy just wanted some coffee. Contemplating the fuss that might occur if he turned the guy in, Craig decided to let the poor man be. There were too many homeless people in the world nowadays. If one of them had found a way to beat the cold desert nights, more power to him.

As he neared the women again, Craig noticed that Lyssa looked as worn-out as he felt. It couldn't be easy reliving that nightmare every time she had to tell it anew. How he wanted to take her in his arms and comfort her. And so much more.

Roxanne lifted a suspicious brow at him, as if she'd read this thought, and Craig felt the coffee mix with a swirl of guilt in his belly. So far, his plan to get Lyssa out of his system was a complete bust.

Watching her with her grandmother and mother only pointed out more clearly how close she was to her family. He respected that. Family ought to be a person's number-one priority. But he wished she'd quit casting grateful glances his way. He was feeling like a cad.

The nurse approached, drawing their attention. "I'm not certain what the cause, but Ms. DeHaviland is resting better than she has in days. Why don't you all go home and do the same. I'll call if matters reverse themselves for the worse, but I don't expect that will be the case."

"The Purity..." Craig implored, his eyes on Lyssa.

"Of course." Lyssa informed the nurse that she needed to visit Grandy's room a moment. She returned two minutes later with Craig's briefcase in tow. He checked the contents, then locked the case and chained it to his wrist.

"Grandy's breathing easier, Mom. She seems to be sleeping like a baby."

"Thank Heaven."

And Craig Rival's generosity, Lyssa thought.

In the elevator, Roxanne asked, "How long are you staying, Mr. Rival?"

Craig realized he hadn't thought beyond tonight. Idella DeHaviland was at death's door; he hadn't counted on her slamming it in the Grim Reaper's face. What if she rallied, went into remission? What if she didn't? Torn, he made a decision. "I'm returning to Seattle tomorrow evening."

"With the Purity?" Roxanne inquired, as the elevator stopped at the lobby.

Of course with the Purity. She didn't really think he'd leave it here, did she? Nor could she expect him to stay indefinitely. He had an office to run. His uncle was no longer there to do it for him, and although Stacey might be perfectly capable of handling things another few days, he hadn't even told her he'd be away. "When I return to Seattle, the Purity will go with me."

Roxanne's expression was hard. She hadn't liked his answer, but she didn't try to change his mind, and he was grateful for that. They walked to the parking lot in silence. A light rainfall had started, filling the air with the scent of wet dirt.

"If you haven't arranged for a motel, you're welcome to stay at my home, Mr. Rival," Roxanne offered.

He smiled at her, certain she'd like nothing better than to pick his brain about Lyssa and wear down his defenses about the Purity. She didn't trust him. Didn't like him. Probably blamed his family for the attack on Lyssa at his house and thought it only right that he had shown up with the Purity as a form of amends. But most of all, she didn't like his interest in Lyssa.

Or was it Lyssa's interest in *him?*

He doubted much got past the lady, and figured he was going to have to stay one jump ahead of her. Giving her a pleasant smile, he said, "I appreciate the offer, but I have a reservation a few blocks from here. Lyssa is going to drop me off. I'll see you tomorrow?"

"Count on it." She gave Lyssa a hug. "Good night, darlin' mine. If you need me—for any reason—call."

THEY'D GONE ABOUT A BLOCK on Desert Drive when Lyssa asked, "Which motel?"

A lighted vacancy sign caught his eye. "That one there."

Lyssa lifted a brow. Wasn't that convenient? she thought, almost laughing as she pulled into the parking space outside the Desert Palm Motel office. Did he really have a room here? Or was he just avoiding the inquisition Mom would have put him through? She studied his sharp features, the yellow porch light pouring through the windshield casting him in an amber glow. Her pulse skipped and her mouth felt dry. Would he kiss her again? Suddenly she didn't want to leave. "Would you like me to pick you up in the morning?"

What he'd have liked was to take her to his room. His blood seemed to run through his veins with the soft thrum of the car motor, and he lifted his hand and traced her jawline, gently pulling her near, rubbing her bottom lip with his thumb. Lyssa closed her eyes. She was lovely in the buttery light. Craig felt his blood heating, tensing with need, the desire so strong he couldn't resist.

Cupping her head in both hands, he brought his lips to hers, tenderly, but the passion exploded, intensifying the wanting to a fierce level. The light inside the car suddenly blossomed to a brilliant beam and Craig and Lyssa jerked apart. A security patrol car was angled at them, headlights and a spotlight aimed inside the car.

Craig got out and explained they were saying good-night and not making some drug deal. Then he leaned inside her window and said, "I can take a cab. And that copy of your agreement with Wayne…could you bring that with you tomorrow?"

It was as if he'd forgotten their moment of passion, as if it had never happened. She felt an odd sense of loss that she knew she shouldn't feel. How could he be so kind and so passionate one minute, and so abrupt the next? "I'll bring you a copy of the agreement. I'll set it out the minute I get home, so that I don't forget. But you won't take a cab anywhere. I'll be here around nine. See you then."

Five minutes later, Lyssa pulled up in front of the two-story stucco house that had served as her business as well as her home for the past three years. It looked dark and deserted, the wrought-iron bars on the windows intimidating. But she couldn't wait to get inside. Hefting the carry-on bag, she raced to the door, and within seconds she was inside, ramming the dead bolt into place and switching on the overhead light.

She spun around to the main room that did double duty as a living room and reception area. Silence surrounded her, and she pressed her back to the door as her glance searched the room. There had been a moment or two when she hadn't thought she'd see this place again, a moment or two when she'd prayed for nothing more than to be within these familiar walls. Now that she was, she felt alone and vulnerable.

Every creak and groan the old house made sounded like an intruder's footsteps. Maybe *she* should have gone home with her mother. It wasn't too late. She could still go there now.

She gripped the carry-on bag to her belly, considering. Her weary body decided the issue. She stepped farther into the living room, cursing the faceless person who had in one night stolen her sense of security. Blast it! She would not be frightened from her own home.

Turning on lights as she went, Lyssa hurried to her workroom. It took several minutes to disengage the alarm system, retrieve from the vault the document that Craig didn't believe existed and reset the security code. Thinking she would have to have the security system installed throughout the house now that she could afford it, Lyssa double-checked all the ground-level windows and doors, then shut off the lights and hastened upstairs to her bedroom.

Nothing scary here, she reassured herself, greeting her enormous doll collection with a "Hello, ladies." Everything was as she'd left it. But maybe a good hot shower would restore her nerves. She discarded her bag on the floor beside a solid brass ginger jar, laid the agreement on her water bed and selected clean panties and a sleep shirt from a bureau drawer. In the bathroom, she turned on the shower and stripped.

LYSSA'S BEDROOM CLOSET door slipped open. The killer crouched among her clothing, listening. The sound of running water gave the intruder, who was dressed like an old man, courage enough to step into the room.

Her bedroom resembled a doll shop, with toys cluttering every corner, perched here and there like watchdogs. *A hundred set of eyes observing my smallest movement. Gives me the willies.* The intruder gave a disgusted grunt. Never liked dolls.

Geez, even the water bed was littered with the creepy things. Something seemed to wave from the center of the bed, paper floating on the pink-and-blue spread. Probably a set of paper dolls. The intruder inched closer. No, it was some sort of legal document. The name Lundeen was prominent, and the intruder leaned over and snatched the paper, then chuckled.

Well, well, would you look at this. It's enough to make my partner forgive me for killing Lyssa. Shoving the paper into a pocket, the killer stared down at the syringe, and again, as in the stairwell at the hospital, considered the difficulties of jabbing Lyssa in a vein. Wasn't likely she would oblige. Couldn't chance any signs of a struggle. But her being in the shower sparked an even better idea. All that was needed was something to conk her with, something unbreakable. Something that would look like she'd slipped and hit her head on the bathtub.

The intruder glanced at the dolls again. Nothing there. But what was that behind the carry-on bag? A brass ginger jar. Perfect. Lifting it, the intruder hurried to the bathroom door, which was ajar.

Lyssa's slender, feminine form was silhouetted through the pastel pink shower curtain. She'd never know what hit her, the intruder thought, grinning at the pun, and stepped through the doorway onto the bath mat, creeping closer, reaching for the shower curtain, the ginger jar raised higher than Lyssa's head.

Chapter Nine

The hot water beat against Lyssa's skin, massaging her aching muscles and easing the tension from her neck and shoulders. Her own bed was going to feel heavenly. If only she could shake the uneasiness that kept creeping over her. Again, she considered packing a small bag and spending the night at her mother's. It was foolish to feel this scared. The house had good locks and she was used to spending the night alone. She shut off the water.

For one whole second, quiet reigned supreme. Oppressive quiet. Then the pipes rattled, water dripped from the shower head, and overriding both, the doorbell rang. *Who in the world would be calling on her at this hour?* Unless . . . Had Grandy gotten worse?

She jerked the shower curtain aside. Oddly, she thought she caught a whiff of whiskey mingled with the scent of shampoo permeating the bathroom. Frowning at her wayward sense of smell, Lyssa snatched a towel, wrapped it around her wet body, then grabbed her robe and shoved her feet into her slippers. She hurried for the staircase, poking her arms into the sleeves of the robe and calling, "I'm coming!"

At the door, she switched on the porch light and peered through the peephole. Her mother. Lyssa's heart stumbled. She snapped the locks free and threw the door wide. "Is it Grandy?"

"No, no." Roxanne gave her a quick hug and moved into the room. She was carrying a tote bag and taking stock of Lyssa's gaping robe, haphazardly draped towel and dripping hair. "No, I presume Mother's maintaining status quo. I was just worried about you. I know how empty a house can be sometimes, especially after the ordeal you've been through, and, well, I thought maybe you'd like some overnight company...unless you already have some?"

Lyssa closed the door and reset the locks. Then, tugging her robe shut, she turned to her mother with a tolerant expression. Did she really think she'd find Craig Rival here? "I'm alone, Mom. And you're more than welcome to stay the night. But only tonight."

In fact, Lyssa was relieved to have her mother here, no matter what had actually brought her.

"Darlin' mine, you are dripping water all over the place. Why don't you go take care of that, while I fix us some hot cocoa?"

"Sounds like a plan." Lyssa smiled at her mother. "But no heart-to-hearts tonight. I'm ready to drop in my tracks."

Her mother looked only slightly disappointed. "Agreed."

Lyssa returned to her room with a lighter step than she'd had earlier. Ten minutes later, her hair wrapped in a towel, she was in the kitchen, wearing her night shirt, and enjoying hot chocolate with her mother.

THE INTRUDER COWERED in the guest bedroom closet, sitting on the floor, back against the wall, legs drawn up, and clutching the brass ginger jar to a heart which only now was slowing to its normal beat. *That was too close. The doorbell startled the daylights out of me. It's a miracle I didn't cry out. Or boggle the whole affair. Instead, I reacted like a coward.* Shame and rage surged through the intruder at the memory.

Damn Lyssa. She ought to be dead, her head cracked open, her lifeblood flowing down the drain. The intruder pictured it and grinned, then, recalling the doorbell, knew the course of action taken had been the smartest one. Couldn't risk hitting her with someone at the door. Lyssa might have screamed, alerting whomever had chosen such a rotten time to show up.

But what now?

Setting the ginger jar on the floor between both legs, the intruder gazed into the upper reaches of the closet. Except for a couple of blankets and pillows on the shelf above the hanger rod, it was empty. And narrow. *Like the linen closet Papa used to lock me in as a kid whenever I was naughty.*

The darkness seemed to press in from all sides. Panic gathered in the intruder's chest and air was gulped instead of inhaled. *Have to get out of the closet.* Gingerly shoving the door aside, the intruder peered out, listening intently.

All was silent. At least, Lyssa wasn't in this room. Moving with slow, deliberate steps, the intruder headed for the bedroom door. A board creaked beneath the Nikes. Wild-eyed, the intruder froze. But no one came to investigate. In the hallway, the sound of voices wafted from below. Her company was still here. Was the other person going to stay long? Long enough to be accused if Lyssa's death didn't appear accidental?

Warming to the thought, the intruder wondered who the visitor was. *Need to get closer.* Down two stairs. *Stop. Listen.* A woman. But who? Did it really matter... as long as Lyssa ended up dead?

For she would die this night. She had to. Failing again would mean putting it off until later in the week. The thought made the intruder's stomach tighten. *I can't chance missing work, can't chance being regarded suspiciously in any way, or for any reason. But the longer Lyssa lives, the greater the risk she will remember seeing me at Windance.*

The voices were coming closer. The intruder hastened into the guest room again and cowered against the wall behind the door.

"The bed has fresh linen. Thanks for coming. I do feel safer now."

That was Lyssa. She and the other woman were on the landing outside the guest room. The intruder's heart thumped

Someone grasped the knob and began pushing the door open. The intruder heard her say, "Sweet dreams, sweetie. I'll see you in the morning."

"'Night, Mom."

Mom? Her mother? Pain twanged the intruder's temples. Who was going to believe her own mother murdered her in the night? Damn! Damn! Double damn! Getting rid of Lyssa was turning into a Chinese puzzle. The intruder dived once again into the dreaded closet, this time leaving the door ajar, but in the haste, the toe of one Nike bumped the abandoned ginger jar, and the resulting clang seemed as loud as a gong. The intruder waited in sheer terror to be discovered, hefting the brass jar high, readied for attack.

But the woman apparently hadn't heard it. She disrobed, pulled back the covers and climbed into bed. The intruder settled on the closet floor and set the jar aside. She'd be asleep soon. Just have to wait. What time was it, anyway? *Wish I could see my watch. It must be after 4:00 a.m.* Stifling a yawn, the intruder slumped against the wall of the closet and closed heavy eyelids.

Sunday

THE ALARM WENT OFF at seven. Lyssa had awakened minutes before, suddenly recalling the agreement. She was certain she'd set it on the bed before taking her shower, but hadn't given it a thought after her mother had arrived. Now she couldn't remember seeing it when she'd slid beneath the covers. She sat up, shuffled through the blankets, then slowly shook each one in turn. Nothing. She scrambled onto her knees and peered over one side of the bed, then the other. Nothing.

With mounting concern, she zipped off the bed and sifted through the dolls she'd scooped onto the floor. Still nothing. A sinking feeling hit her stomach. Impossibly, the agreement was gone.

Lyssa sat there bewildered, her gaze jumping from familiar item to familiar item, when, with a jolt, she realized something else was missing. A clammy sensation swept her as she stared at the empty spot where her brass ginger jar had been last night when she'd dropped her carry-on bag in front of it. The clammy sensation was washed away in a brutal chill as she bolted from her room into the guest bedroom. "Mom!"

Roxanne sprang up, startled from sleep by Lyssa's outcry. "What is it? Mother?"

"No. I just wanted to see if you were all…right…." Lyssa trailed off, stopping dead in her tracks, as her gaze steadied on the open closet door and the missing ginger jar that lay overturned inside.

"Well, I was until you scared the stuffing out of me. Lyssa? Lyssa? Why, what's the matter? You're white as paste."

"Did you take the ginger jar out of my room last night?" But even as she asked, Lyssa knew the answer. Her mother hadn't gone into her room. Had she been so sleepy she'd mistakenly thought she'd seen the ginger jar where it belonged? She couldn't believe that. Yes, she'd been stressed out lately about Grandy, but that didn't explain when or how the jar had gotten into this closet…or the odd whiff of whiskey she'd smelled last night in her bathroom, and she'd swear lingered in the closet now.

Or where the agreement had gone.

Her knees wobbled.

"Lyssa?" Roxanne threw back the covers, grabbed her robe and scurried to her daughter's side.

Lyssa took a deep breath. She didn't want to alarm her mother, but that seemed unavoidable. "I'd suggest you get dressed as fast as possible. I'm going to call the police. Unless I'm very much mistaken, we had an intruder last night."

"What?"

"I'll call from my room. Hurry, get dressed."

But Lyssa didn't make it back to her room without Roxanne. She grabbed her clothes and raced after her daughter. They locked the bedroom door. Roxanne checked the bathroom and the closet, ensuring they were alone. Lyssa, relieved to find the phone working, dialed the police.

By eight-thirty, the police had come and gone. They hadn't found any signs of a break-in. It had rained the night before and there were no footprints outside any windows. If someone had gotten into the house last night, they'd concluded, she'd either let them in or they'd had a key. But the key she'd hidden outside, after twice locking herself out, was still in its place, and a check for fingerprints produced nothing but smudges.

The official hypothesis had seemed to be that since the only item missing was a scrap of paper, it was most likely that she'd mislaid it. However, if she was still concerned, she could change her locks.

After the incident at Windance and now this, Lyssa determined leaving keys outdoors for any reason was not something she'd ever do again. She made arrangements to meet a locksmith at the house later that day. It galled her that the police thought she was paranoid. Someone had been in the house. Someone had moved the ginger jar. Someone had taken the agreement. But why? To discredit her with Craig Rival? For he certainly wasn't going to believe her any more than the police had. She doubted even seeing their official report would satisfy him, but it was tucked inside her purse nonetheless.

He was waiting outside the motel when she drove up, again wearing black jeans, but today his shirt was yellow and black. Her palms were damp, her mouth dry. A sweet tingle of desire spread lazily through her as he climbed into the car. His sensuous after-shave tugged on her senses.

Vulnerable. Personally and professionally. That was the effect he had on her, and she hated it. She liked being the one in control. Steeling herself against his immediate request for the agreement, she was relieved when he didn't mention it. They drove to the hospital, conversing about Superstition Mountain and the beauty of Arizona in September.

ROXANNE WAS NOT ALONE in the waiting room. Her two younger brothers sat on either side of her. Lyssa's stomach did a slow roll. But her mother had apparently already told them both to expect Craig. Although she was greeted with hugs and kisses, he was given a lukewarm reception. Lyssa strove to break the tension. "How's Grandy?"

"It's incredible." There was a brightness in her mother's eyes she hadn't seen in awhile. "We're waiting for the doctor to confirm it, but the nurse suspects she's going into another remission. Keep your fingers crossed."

Half an hour later, the doctor, more prudently than the nurse, told them that Idella did seem more alert, her spirits good, but cautioned them against thinking remission without some solid proof. He'd know more in a few days.

But if looks were any indication, Grandy was indeed feeling better. The moment she saw Craig and Lyssa, she shooed her sons and daughter from her side and asked, "Did you bring my necklace?" Her voice was stronger than it had been in weeks.

Craig quickly produced it from the briefcase and presented it to her.

Idella, propped up by extra pillows at her back, accepted the Purity with reverence, as though she'd accepted a dried rose petal that might disintegrate if she breathed on it. Her gnarled fingers caressed each stone, every ounce of gold. Then she lifted it to her neck, insisted Lyssa fasten it and demanded a mirror. The blue of the diamonds stood out against the pale hospital gown, giving the ocean blue eyes a deep pure clarity. Idella gazed at herself, her expression becoming dreamy, as if she were remembering a time when she was young, her neck as smooth and lovely as the necklace.

Craig was reminded of his mother.

"You look beautiful, Grandy," Lyssa said.

Idella smiled at her. "No, this is a young woman's necklace. A bride's necklace. But I am happy. And that is your doing, Lyssa. Yours...and this young man of yours." She gazed at Craig now, studying him as if something about him were familiar, something she couldn't quite put her finger on.

It gave Lyssa a moment of concern. Did Craig resemble his grandfather? Was Grandy seeing family similarities?

"Have we met before, young man?"

Lyssa blanched. "Grandy, this is Craig . . . uh—"

"Smith," Roxanne finished for her.

Ignoring the scowl on her uncles' faces, Lyssa watched Craig's neck grow red and guessed even this necessary lie would bode poorly for her honesty.

Grandy seemed to notice Lyssa's dismay. She frowned at her reprovingly. "Don't you fret, girl. Nothing wrong with the name Smith. It's good, honest, all-American."

"I . . . agree," Lyssa sputtered.

"And a mighty handsome devil he is, too." Grandy smiled. "I can finally go to my reward knowing my Lyssa will have a good and lasting marriage. Welcome to the family, Craig Smith. Now come here and give an old lady a kiss on the cheek."

Silence charged the air. Lyssa couldn't believe she'd heard right. Where had her grandmother gotten such an idea? Heat burned her face. She avoided looking at her mother and her uncles.

Craig was embarrassed also, but he obliged Idella DeHaviland with a kiss on the cheek and then started to step back.

Idella grasped his wrist. "Not so quick. Here undo the clasp." With obvious effort, she shifted on the bed to accommodate him. Her breathing seemed louder. "I might not make it to your wedding, so I want to see you put the Purity on Lyssa, here and now."

Craig bit down his chagrin and glanced at Lyssa. Her face was the shade of rubies, but her eyes were filled with concern. He could feel her silent plea to go along with anything as long as it didn't upset her grandmother. The rest of her family seemed just as eager that he comply. Craig balked at the idea. Letting Idella believe they were getting married was downright cruel. She'd have to learn the truth sooner or later.

Before he could voice his protest, Lyssa was at his side, staring up at him with those bedeviling eyes. "It's okay, darling—I don't mind, really."

Against his better judgment, Craig undid the clasp, then placed the necklace around Lyssa's neck, leaning near, breathing in the heady scent of her delicate perfume. He felt suddenly clumsy, his fingers all thumbs, brushing her soft skin. Shivers of desire raced through him.

"Let's see you," Grandy said. Her voice had grown weaker, but her gaze was eager. "Oh my, oh my, oh my. Look at how beautiful the blue of the necklace is with her complexion, with her eyes. Oh my, yes. Now, Craig, you must kiss your bride."

Craig arched a brow at Lyssa, who was still reeling from their slight physical contact. What would a kiss do to them? She knew it would have more impact than it had at the funeral, more impact than last night. And that scared her.

Roxanne stepped forward, and snapped in exasperation, "Really, Mother. Is that really necessary?"

"Yes, Roxanne, it is. For me." Grandy laid her head against the pillows.

Lyssa could see she was tiring. "You need some rest, Grandy. We'll come back later."

"Please, Lyssa," Grandy said, her voice thin and reedy. "Every time I fall asleep there's the chance I won't awaken."

The words were a harsh reminder that hopes of a remission were premature, without foundation. Lyssa's throat tightened, and her stomach felt full of rocks.

"Please, give me something sweet to see when I close my eyes. Let me dream of the wedding I may not live to attend."

The wedding I may not live to attend. It was the last thing Craig's mother had said to him as she bestowed the Purity into his safekeeping for the daughter-in-law she would never meet.

Heedless of all else, Craig pulled Lyssa into his arms and lowered his lips to hers. Even though this was the third time he'd kissed her, he was unprepared for the jolt of desire that rocketed the length of him as their mouths melded into a sensuous kiss, a kiss meant to be brief, a kiss that lasted long enough to pull a sigh from Lyssa and command his strongest effort at self-control in all his thirty years. They parted breathlessly, staring at one another as if no one else were in the room.

Grandy's chuckle was as soft as a baby chick's peep. "At long last, Roxanne, our Lyssa will be happy."

"We're going now, Mother." Roxanne's face was pale and pinched. She caught hold of Lyssa by the elbow. "We'll be back this afternoon."

Lyssa shook off her mother's hold, undid the necklace's clasp and handed Craig the Purity. He appeared as confused and as flustered by their kiss as she was. The first time had been nothing like this. Even the second time had not prepared her for the truth. There were serious feelings between them, feelings that begged to be unleashed. Heaven knew she was willing. Heaven knew she shouldn't be.

Her uncles glared at Craig, then at her, before leaving the room. From the doorway, Roxanne said, "Lyssa, Grandy needs her rest."

Lyssa kissed her grandmother, then joined her mother and uncles in the hallway as Craig placed the Purity in the briefcase. She kept her voice low. "Save your breath. I don't need a lecture on the Rival clan from any of you."

Her uncles reminded her that she knew the score in that arena, and left. Roxanne was not so easily dismissed. Her hands were on her hips. "No lectures. Just tell me what's going on between the two of you."

How could she tell her mother something she didn't understand? How could she tell her mother that kissing this man set her body on fire? Made her want to follow him to the ends of the earth? Why incur her mother's wrath? "Nothing's going on. He's merely a very nice man, doing a very nice deed. Why can't you leave it at that?"

Roxanne sighed loudly, impatiently. "Darlin' mine, I've seen the way that man looks at you—not to mention the way you look at him. And that kiss! You're still blushing from it. If you think nothing's going on between you, then you're not using the brains God gave you, and the common sense your Dad and I instilled."

Craig came out of the room. Roxanne gave a disgusted "humph" and stormed away.

He didn't ask what the matter was. He knew. Roxanne DeHaviland and her brothers wanted him as far away from Lyssa as he could get. So would Idella if she knew his true identity. As for him, he'd had enough of the DeHaviland family to last him aeons. He sure as hell didn't want to be attracted to Lyssa. But, he was. More now than when he'd gotten on the plane with her. More now than he'd been to any woman as far back as he could remember.

Totally embarrassed about her family's behavior, Lyssa could barely look Craig in the eye. Or maybe it was her reaction to their kisses that had her feeling like a schoolgirl. Her blood was still heated. She didn't want to be attracted to him, but she was. More than when she'd left Seattle. More than she'd been to any man as far back as she could remember.

But nothing would come of it. Her family had just made that painfully clear. They would never accept him. Besides, infatuation—even out-and-out love— was a risky proposition. She needed only to look at Kevin and herself, and at the war zone her parents had called marriage. No, even if Craig were not a Rival, she could only get hurt encouraging this budding desire for him.

"I'm s-sorry," she stammered, "for lying about your name, for Grandy assuming we're . . . you know, for the bit about the wedding, and for Mom's rudeness, and...oh, for everything. I know we haven't been fair to you, haven't exactly treated your kind deed with the gratitude it and you deserve, but I will always be indebted to you."

Guilt swept through Craig like a nasty wind. He didn't want her gratitude. He didn't deserve it. Not really. Not when what he wanted right now was her. Not when he didn't even understand why he wanted a woman who'd done nothing but perplex him from their first encounter.

Maybe he'd better go home and regroup. "Apologies aren't necessary. But you're going to have to tell your grandmother the truth. I'm leaving tonight. With the Purity. With my copy of your agreement with Wayne." He stopped, cocking his head to one side. "Do you have that, by the way?"

Lyssa felt the heat rising into her cheeks. "Um...you're probably not going to believe this, but..." She explained about the break-in, showed him the police report and swore she had the document the previous evening that she'd gotten it out of her safe and laid it on the bed.

"I don't believe this. Why can't you just tell me the truth?" How many times had she asked him to believe her without proof? Three, four, five? He'd lost count. All tangible evidence, including the scene in her grandmother's sickroom, verified that she was a liar.

"But I am telling you the truth."

Growling with frustration, Craig spun away from her, then quickly back. "Look, I can't allow myself to be dragged further into this mess of yours. I have a business to run in Seattle. I'm glad your grandmother is doing better, but you'll have to straighten her out about us, and about the Purity."

"Of course. But I'm not lying about the agreement. Or about the faux Purity. You must believe me. Let me drive you to the airport. We'll straighten this out."

"No thanks. I'll call a cab."

Lyssa just stared at him. What was it with this man? One minute he was kissing her, the next calling her a liar. Granted he had cause, but still, why the sudden rush to be away from her? Was he afraid of their feelings for one another? Or was there something here she hadn't considered?

An awful thought occurred to her. What if he'd been the one who'd stolen the agreement? He could have had time to get to her house and into her room while she was in the shower. Had he done that? She stepped away from him, her stomach feeling queasy. Was he somehow involved in the attacks on her?

Craig didn't seem to notice her retreat. "If you are truly indebted to me, please prove it by staying out of my life."

Chapter Ten

Friday

"Not even the threat of burglary could dissuade Craig Rival from his mission." The sarcasm in Stacey Rival's comment was swallowed in the swish of silk lining as she donned her black raincoat, a designer original she wore regardless of the weather.

Craig glanced toward the showroom windows. The sky was clear, a brilliant blue almost as dazzling as the Purity. He gazed again at his stepcousin, who was wrapping the coat's belt around her small waist. "There will always be thieves, but I won't have them ruling my life. Not for one minute. That's what security systems are for. The Collection goes back in its case. Now."

"Just in time for C.J.'s visit," Stacey said, as if C.J. Temple's appointment with Craig were the motive behind his insistence on setting up the display. She gathered her briefcase and purse and headed for the outer door. "Give my best to C.J. With any luck, I won't be back until after she's gone."

"Stacey," Craig called, stopping her. Without removing her hand from the doorknob, she glanced over her shoulder. Was the animosity in her outlandishly made-up hazel eyes for C.J. or him? She'd been sullen since the reading of Wayne's will, since her discovery that her father's newly acquired partnership hadn't automatically reverted to her on his death, and her attitude had given Craig a dreadful week of hashing and rehashing the accusations Lyssa had made about her... and about David. If only he hadn't broached the subject with Stacey this morning.... She'd been furious. The glare she gave him said she still was. "Did C.J. say what she wanted?"

"Ginger took the call." Stacey nodded toward the salesclerk coming from the inner offices, balancing jewelry boxes like a waitress in some greasy-spoon diner.

Craig swore. His outcry startled Ginger. The boxes of precious merchandise wobbled. He rushed to help, tamping down his irritation.

The muted gong sounded.

Glancing toward the door, he saw Stacey had gone. Probably straight to David. He slid boxes onto the counter and blew out a frustrated sigh. He had the awful feeling this was not going to be a good day. "Did C.J. Temple mention any piece in particular when she set up her appointment?"

"Nope. Just said she and her assistant would be here at one." Ginger's face was bright pink, as if she were flustered. She hurried back to the vault.

Craig grabbed up a dust cloth and crossed to the handsome display case his father had had built to specification twenty years earlier. Arcs of sunlight spotlighted its aged beauty and emphasized its emptiness. That emptiness offended him. He unlocked the back panel and swept the cloth through the inside shelf before covering it with a length of black velvet.

Ginger deposited more boxes on the counter.

Craig set the diamond- and ruby-studded Russian czarina's tiara centermost on the length of velvet, positioned an eighteenth-century broach beside it, then continued placing the treasured pieces in the order that he liked them.

"Here." Ginger proffered the Purity, smiling at him, reminding him unexpectedly of Lyssa. He felt as if he'd been hit in the gut. "Where are you going to put it?" she asked.

Staring at the Purity, he heard Idella DeHaviland calling it the wedding necklace. His stomach turned. In spite of her hostility toward his family, he couldn't help worrying about the grand old gal. He'd phoned the hospital every day, checking on her condition, and was relieved to hear she was improving.

He wished he could say the same for his confusion over Lyssa. If anything, it was getting worse. Over the past six days, he'd found himself pondering again and again the question of why she'd lied to him about the document, even after he'd brought the Purity for her grandmother's sake. Not one believable answer had occurred to him. And yet he was still seeking answers, or he wouldn't have confronted Stacey today.

Craig settled the Purity on the velvet. The weighty piece of precious stone and metal was worth more to him than all the other treasures in the case combined. At least his family had carried on the original tradition. One day, his wedding day, he'd present it to his wife...and that woman sure as blazes wouldn't be Lyssa Carlyle. The DeHavilands would never accept such a union. Since the loss of his parents, family was wholly important to him, and, if humanly possible, he wanted in-laws who'd welcome him into hearth and home.

Besides, he'd told Lyssa to stay out of his life. He'd meant it.

STAY OUT OF MY LIFE. Craig's words rang inside Lyssa's head as she hurried across the lobby of Seattle's Four Seasons Hotel and into the crunch of other conventioneers waiting to board the elevators. As much as she'd have liked to oblige Craig—and her family—she couldn't stay out of his life.

Grandy's needs had to come before all else. Although the doctor agreed she seemed better, he was annoyingly cautious about her improvement. *I'll know more in a few days.*

But how many days did Grandy have?

Jostling her luggage, she pictured her grandmother propped against the pillows of her hospital bed, looking frail, asking for the Purity, asking to see Craig Smith. Lyssa flushed in shame. It had seemed such a necessary, innocent lie at the time. But almost immediately it had doubled, then tripled, until now the truth was buried under so much fertilizer it could grow flowers.

She winced at the thought of how putrid those flowers would smell. Lies and secrets had a way of poking through the soil and reaching for the light of day, usually to the dismay of the devious gardeners who'd nurtured them.

If only she could tell Grandy the truth. The elevator arrived and carried her to the tenth floor. But what if the truth zapped her newfound will to live? The possibility tore at Lyssa. Whether or not she convinced Craig that a faux Purity existed, she was bent on persuading him to let her make another.

In her room, she unpacked hurriedly, chose an outfit that might help win him over and changed clothes. He would not be happy to see her. Probably wouldn't want to listen. Well, she'd just have to think of something.

But a half hour later she still had no solid plan as she headed out to the street. The crisp air had a refreshing tang—a pinch of salt water, a dash of exhaust and a dollop of autumn. It was the kind of day when being alive felt wonderful, when nothing bad could happen. Lyssa decided she'd walk the few blocks to Rival Gems International.

After all the hours she'd spent at the hospital the past week, stretching her legs on these hills felt grand. She shared the sidewalks with intent executives hurrying to or from lunches, tourists complaining about the price of lunch and street people wishing for any kind of lunch, wishing they could switch places with those more fortunate....

Switch places!

She stopped dead in her tracks. A woman rammed into her, muttered something obscene, then joined the other pedestrians streaming around her.

Of course. Now she knew why the genuine Purity had turned up, but not the copy, knew why someone had stolen the document—the only corroborating piece of proof of the faux's existence—from her house.

Her heart thundered inside her chest. Someone was planning to switch the two necklaces, just biding their time until Craig's guard was completely down, or until he was away on another of his buying trips, before implementing their plan. Whoever it was must be hoping they'd get lucky, counting on no one paying particularly close attention to the necklace as long as it was in its place in the Collection showcase.

Craig *had* to believe the copy existed. Before the Purity was stolen. She picked up her pace, and was soon headed downhill for the waterfront area.

Lyssa had gone less than three blocks when the odd sense that someone was watching—following—hit her. The same feeling she'd had at the airport and at Wayne's funeral. Was the person who'd attacked her at Windance coming after her again? She forced herself to keep moving, but her feet were starting to ache in the high-heeled shoes, and haste was nearly impossible. Why hadn't she worn her sneakers? She'd gone a short block farther when the sensation struck her again—that eyes-drilling-into-the-back-of-her-head feeling. Fighting off panic, she spun around. Scanned faces. Everywhere she looked—strangers. What was she looking for? She'd never seen her attacker's face.

Keep going! She hurried on, trying to calm herself. Maybe she was overreacting. Maybe she was being foolish.

Better foolish than dead.

She swallowed hard. Dead. Someone had tried twice to kill her. It was a thought she'd shoved aside. It came back now with the force of floodwater. Why? What possible threat could she be to anyone? There was only her word that the faux Purity existed, and no one who mattered believed her. There had to be another reason. Did she know something—had she seen something—that was worth killing her for?

Streets and sidewalks were awash with people and cars, voices and motors. An anxious knot grabbed her stomach, and she was breathing hard when she drew abreast of Craig's building. The waterfront, briny and rank, saturated her every breath.

Frantic, she headed into the alley separating Madison and Spring Avenues, scanning the back of the building, seeking an entrance to the brick structure. Nearer the other end of the alley, she spotted a glass door. *Please, God, let it be a back entrance.*

As if in answer to her prayer, a slender blonde dressed in a suit similar to her own came through the door and strode leisurely into the alley, glancing at her wristwatch. Lyssa broke into a run. Her high heel dipped into a hole. The heel snapped. Her ankle wrenched. Pain shot up her left leg. Wincing, she hopped to the side of the building and bent over, clutching the injured ankle.

A piercing squeal of tires rent the air. Lyssa lurched around. A minivan careened into the alley. Tires yelped. The engine revved. Horror-stricken, Lyssa froze. The van picked up speed, roaring straight for her.

Chapter Eleven

Standing to one side, Craig watched C.J. Temple and
Teri Dean wander the showroom, perusing the display cases. C.J. lingered over the Collection as if it
were a picnic spread for her indulgence, something
ironically akin to Stacey's suggestion. Teri demon-
strated more interest in the Markum Estate pieces.

Craig glanced at his watch, wondering how long
C.J. would continue this posturing. Perhaps he should
take the initiative and get the meeting underway. He
moved toward her, thinking that for all her understated elegance, she reminded him of a fox, parading
past the display cases as if they held fat hens, one of
which she would snatch and carry off for supper.

She gazed up at him. Her eyes had the lumines-
cence of the very predator he'd likened her to, heated,
watchful, cunning. Craig tensed. "Do you have a
buyer for one of our recent acquisitions, C.J.?"

"Nothing so mundane." Her voice was pleasantly
husky, but she wasn't a woman who wasted her time
flirting. He didn't doubt the rumors of her sexual
prowess, but she wouldn't have to seek out the
younger men she supposedly preferred. This fox would

attract them like hunters. She laid her eel-skin brief-case on the Collection case. "My buyer is interested in something closer to your own heart."

Unaccountably, his mouth went dry. "And what might that be?"

"The Purity."

Surprise arrowed through him. A number of reasons for this meeting had occurred to him. None included an offer for the Purity. He glanced over his shoulder at Teri. Her face went instantly red, as if he'd caught her pocketing one of the Markum Estate broaches. He folded his arms across his chest and stared down at C.J. "The Purity is not for sale. You know perfectly well that nothing in that case is."

"My client is willing to pay more than it's worth." Her tone indicated he'd be a fool not to hear her out.

He'd rather throw her out. But he hesitated, sensing Teri's eyes on him, sensing her tension. He clamped his jaw as an errant thought struck him. Was the client . . . Lyssa? He had told her to stay out of his life, which would keep the Purity out of *her* life. Perhaps her old friend Teri had helped devise a scheme to get it back. Curious, he asked, "How much is 'more than it's worth'?"

C.J. named a price that would ensure a commission large enough to keep her in French and Italian couturier suits—like the dove gray one she wore now—for many years.

Craig smiled, an indulgent lifting of the corners of his mouth.

C.J. upped the ante.

Craig was impressed, but not swayed. "Who is this generous client of yours, C.J.?"

Lifting her eyebrows, she unzipped the briefcase, withdrew a scrap of paper and scrawled on it. "My buyers pay for my discretion, and this one insists on remaining anonymous."

Craig would just bet she did.

C.J. offered the scrap of paper to him. "This is as high as I'm authorized to go."

Craig let out a low whistle of appreciation, but shook his head. "You can't buy sentiment."

"Sentiment?" C.J. snorted, and a contemptuous sneer robbed her face of youth. "What a softhearted, softheaded load of crap. I'll tell you what sentiment will get you, mister—months of living on cat food, doctor bills galore, a medical health-care system more interested in dollars than human beings, and finally a death that robs you of your last shred of dignity."

Stepping back as if she'd struck him, Craig blinked at C.J. Where had that come from? Deep inside her soul, apparently. A person would have to have lived that kind of tragedy to speak of it with the vehemence C.J. had.

With her lips drawn into a thin white line, she whirled away from him.

So...C.J. had a weak spot, one she regretted showing him, one that explained the driving force behind her ruthless business techniques. He regarded her expensive clothing again, her pristine lack of jewelry. The suit wasn't new, but the style was timeless. It declared C.J. Temple wouldn't choose material items for frivolity or indulgence, and, Craig figured, it was probably a safe bet she had her own future secured. Or was working on it.

Obviously embarrassed by her outburst, C.J. busied herself rezipping her briefcase. Teri, he noticed, had resumed her interest in the Markum Estate. He strode to her side, and was relating a story about one of the rings, wishing they were alone and he could question her about Lyssa, when the gong sounded and Ginger came in.

Breathless, as if she were late, she nodded at C.J. and Teri, then disappeared into the back room.

C.J. had regained her composure. "If you change your mind, Craig..."

But before Craig could tell her that wasn't going to happen, the muted gong sounded again. This time David and Stacey came through the foyer door. Stacey's face was even more bloodless than usual.

Craig braced himself, hoping neither would bring up Lyssa and what he'd discussed with Stacey this morning—not in front of C.J. and Teri.

Instead, David said, "There was a hit-and-run in the alley out back."

"Didn't you hear the ambulance and the sirens?" Stacey wailed.

But they'd heard nothing. This room was soundproof.

"It's unbelievable," David said, helping Stacey out of her raincoat and into a chair. "A couple of women were run down. One of them was that Lyssa Carlyle."

Teri gasped.

Craig thought his heart had stopped. Lyssa? What was she doing here? Outside this building? Run down?

"Is she...?"

Ginger stood in the doorway to the back room, her eyes wide, her face pale, apparently waiting for an answer to the same question.

David shrugged. "All we know is that they've been taken to Virginia Mason."

Stacey seemed to be still seeing the horror. "There's blood all over the pavement."

Ginger jammed her hand against her mouth as if to stifle an outcry.

"Oh, my God." Teri hurried for the door. "C.J., I'll call you from the hospital."

"I'm coming too." Ginger ignored Teri's obvious discomfort at the suggestion and hurried into the back room, emerging a second later with her coat and purse.

Craig was opening the door for them. "I'll drive you," he insisted, not caring that his cousin and his lawyer and C.J. were gaping at him in total surprise.

Minutes later, the Lexus was speeding up Spring Avenue, racing for the Virginia Mason Medical Center.

The tension inside the car was palpable. Craig had wanted an opportunity to ask Teri whether or not Lyssa was the buyer C.J. had for the Purity. Now he no longer cared. *God, don't let her injuries be serious. Or fatal.*

His pulse thumped against his temples, and his scalp prickled. Sitting beside him, Teri seemed in as bad shape as he. Her eyes looked huge and hollow, and her thin mouth dipped toward her chin, pulling deep grooves in her cheeks. In the rearview mirror, he could see Ginger was chewing a nail to the quick. He wished he could tell them Lyssa would be all right, but he couldn't get Stacey's words about the blood on the pavement out of his head.

AT THE HOSPITAL THEY WERE told that Lyssa was unconscious, undergoing tests. Ginger went to find a telephone.

Relegated to a waiting room, Craig paced like a caged tiger, barely aware of the fearful expressions of the young man and older woman seated in the corner, not even noticing Teri leave, until she returned with two disposable cups of coffee.

Handing him one, she said, "I know, caffeine as a tranquilizer is irrational...."

She trailed off. Craig didn't answer. The wheels of his mind were churning like the fear in his gut. Was this a third attempt on Lyssa's life? Was this his fault for talking to Stacey? Like a voracious insect, the notion gnawed through his long-held perceptions of his cousin and his lawyer, shredding his respect, his trust of them. A sour taste layered his tongue. Was he the betrayer or the betrayed? Were David and Stacey undeserving of his suspicions? Had they witnessed the aftermath of the accident, as they'd claimed? His jaw clenched. Or had one or both of them been in the vehicle that had run the two women down?

Ginger returned, and Craig was glad for anything that pulled him away from his ugly musings. "Did you call your family?"

"What? Oh, no. Not yet." She glanced uneasily at Teri. "I hoped to have something to tell them first. Have you heard anything more?"

"No." Why didn't someone tell them something? His grip tightened dangerously on the soft cup. "What's taking so long?"

A female doctor entered, dressed in surgical wear. Craig looked up expectantly, but the grim-faced surgeon stepped past him toward the couple in the corner. The news for these people would not be good. Would there soon be similar news of Lyssa? His heart raced. He set his coffee on an end table and started out of the room. "I'll see what I can find out."

A male doctor, whose hairline and waistline had slipped, blocked his path. "Lyssa Carlyle's family?"

"Here," Ginger said in a squeak.

"How is she?" Panic squeezed Craig's chest. "Is she going to be all right?"

The doctor regarded him with a flicker of curiosity. "She's got a mild concussion and a wrenched ankle, but otherwise she'll be fine."

"Thank God!" Craig was amazed at the jubilation he heard in his own voice, amazed at the intensity of relief washing through him. When had Lyssa Carlyle crept under his skin and into his heart? *But what about the blood Stacey claimed covered the alley?* The doctor had mentioned nothing about cuts. "I thought Lyssa was hit by a car."

The doctor lowered his voice. "The other young woman." He gestured toward the couple leaving with the surgeon. The gray-haired woman held on to the young man as if she were attached to his side, moving clumsily, weeping softly against his arm.

Craig felt a lump the size of a tennis ball in his throat. It might have been Lyssa. If he was right, it was supposed to have been Lyssa.

Teri drew the doctor's attention. "Can we see Ms. Carlyle?"

"The police are with her now, but they should be done soon."

"Well," Ginger said the second the doctor had strolled from the room. "I'll get back to the office."

Craig stopped her. "I think your boss can spare you the afternoon, under the circumstances." She was related to Lyssa, after all. It would be more appropriate if he left, but he wasn't budging and he didn't care what either of them—or anyone else—thought about it. "Surely you want to see your cousin."

Ginger looked completely flustered. "No, really, I have some phone calls—"

"Call from here—"

"I'd rather not." Ginger hurried from the waiting room, squelching any further protest.

Craig glanced at Teri. "What was that all about?"

She shook her head and sighed. "Who knows."

But Teri did know. Craig could see that, and he could see she had no intention of satisfying his curiosity.

"You don't have to stay on my account," she said. "I can take a taxi, or even walk back to my office."

"That's all right. I want to talk to Lyssa."

Teri arched one brow, interest filling her soft blue eyes. Craig took a swallow of coffee and sank to the plastic sofa. She wouldn't satisfy his curiosity, so why should he satisfy hers?

LYSSA FELT AS IF she'd rammed her head into a concrete wall, but she thanked heaven for every throbbing, thumping ache. The other woman would never ache again; the image of her body flying over the minivan like a jettisoned pilot flashed into Lyssa's mind. She blinked against the sudden onslaught of dizziness. And fear.

"Your pulse is a bit erratic." The nurse holding her wrist was frowning. "Try and relax."

Relax? At the moment, that was as impossible as thinking clearly. She'd remembered being followed. The police officer had listened, quietly taking notes, then declared that she hadn't been the one run down, that only bad timing had put her on the spot.

She knew he was wrong.

But she'd been unable to make him understand. Words jumbled inside her head and came out wrong. If only she hadn't fainted, hadn't banged her noggin on the pavement. If only she didn't have this headache. She closed her eyes, but a man's voice brought them flashing open. Was it really... "Craig?"

"Feeling up to some company?"

"Please." Lyssa's heartbeat quickened. How had he known to come? Anxious to speak to him, she pushed up from the pillows. Dizziness attacked, robbing her words and blurring her vision, and all that came out was a groan.

"I know just how you're feeling," Craig said. She grimaced, pain flickering in her eyes. Rage boiled inside him. He wanted the person who'd done this to her, who'd killed that other young woman. Who'd meant to kill Lyssa.

Her vision cleared as he walked to the edge of the bed, his gaze locked with hers. He looked wonderful; his blue-black hair was disheveled, his enticing mouth puckered in a frown, his dark brown eyes full of concern. She felt encouraged. Maybe she could make him believe the danger she was in. That the Purity was in. "Craig, I have to tell you—"

"Hello, lady." Teri peered around Craig. "How are you feeling?"

"Teri?" Startled, Lyssa flinched and pain zipped around her skull. She winced. "How...?"

"I was at Rival Gems."

"Oh."

"C.J. had business with Craig." Teri's face pinkened, and her eyes darted nervously, guiltily.

Despite his worry, Craig again found himself wondering if Lyssa was the client C.J. had for the Purity.

Teri moved toward the bed. "The doctor thinks they'll be releasing you tomorrow. Why don't you come and spend the rest of the weekend at my apartment?"

"Thanks, but..." Lyssa's voice sounded as weak as she felt. "Have speech tomorrow...at conference."

Craig spoke before Teri could respond. "Would you like me to contact someone at the Four Seasons and cancel that for you?"

"No thanks.... I'll manage it."

But would she? he wondered. Would she be allowed to even leave here alive? "Do the police know who did this?"

"No, but I gave...description...van."

Craig stood as stiff as a board. "Did you see the driver?"

"No...police said hit...run...hard to prove."

Which meant the maniac after Lyssa would get away—yet again. Cold swept Craig.

Teri touched the back of Lyssa's hand with a fingertip. "I'm just grateful that you're going to be all right."

Lyssa smiled. "Me, too."

"You're looking awfully tired, and I have to get back to the office, but I'll be in Seattle on Sunday afternoon, at Pike Place Market. Maybe we can get together. I'll meet you for dinner or lunch or just coffee. So call, okay?"

"Sure."

Teri glanced at Craig. "Are you coming?"

"Not just yet."

"Oh?" Teri was openly curious.

But Craig owed her no explanations. "If you need money for a cab..."

"No, no, I can manage." She backed reluctantly from the room. "Thanks for the lift."

As soon as Teri was gone, Craig returned to Lyssa's bedside. How did he broach this subject without further alarming her?

She spared him the trouble. "Not a random hit...run. Someone was following me."

Craig's neck prickled, the same creepy sensation he'd had in Belmont when he'd wondered how the attacks on Lyssa at Windance could have been random. Now he knew they weren't. "Did you see who it was?"

She swallowed as if there was something stuck in her throat. "No. But I sensed them watching...all the way...from hotel to your building."

There was a pleading look in her eyes. Craig nodded. "I believe you."

A sigh of relief slipped from Lyssa, and she leaned back on the pillows, closing her eyes momentarily. "Thank you."

He waited until she seemed ready. "Were you coming to see me?"

"Yes. About Purity. Figured out why the faux and my agreement with Wayne were stolen."

Craig could not look at her injured face and keep denying to himself that both of these items existed. "Why?"

"Someone is planning . . . to steal the Purity."

"You'd better explain."

Haltingly, Lyssa told him of her conclusion that someone intended switching the two necklaces. It made sense. But why these attempts to eliminate her? Unless . . . "Do you know who plans to steal the Purity?"

She drew a ragged breath. "No."

"But the person must suspect you know."

Fear swam in her eyes. "I guess."

"Did you tell this to the police officer?"

"No. But I told him I was being followed. He didn't believe me."

Lyssa seemed to be growing steadier with each statement.

"That settles it, then. You're not staying here. I'll send the nurse in to help you dress, then I'll find your doctor and get you checked out."

AN HOUR LATER, Craig had her settled in his condo, in one of his black T-shirts, in his bed. "If you need anything . . ."

"I'd like to talk a minute." Lyssa inched over and gestured for him to sit on the bed.

He hesitated.

"I'm getting a crick in my neck from staring up at you."

"You promised you were going to stay out of my life," he whispered huskily, as, against his better judgment, he sank cautiously to the bed and gently lifted a lock of her golden hair. His fingers grazed her warm skin and his gaze traced her face, as if she were some precious gem he'd just discovered. "And now, here you are . . . in my bed."

Lyssa's heart did a slow roll. Craig smelled wonderful—of spicy after-shave and coffee. Unbidden, her gaze fell to his mouth, and her throat constricted as she remembered the feel of that mouth on hers. "I never promised."

"Of course you did." Even with a purple goose egg marring her forehead, this woman enticed him. Perhaps it was her sea green eyes, as mystically warm and inviting as forbidden pools. Or her pouty lips. Instantly he recalled the taste of those lips, recalled the tingling sensation that had shot through him each time he'd kissed them, the sensation that was shooting through him now. "I remember."

"I—"

Craig's face dipped toward hers, cutting off her words, her thoughts. And then he was feathering his lips over hers, tentatively, cautiously, as if he needed proof she was really alive, as if she were so fragile she'd break at his touch. Ripples of desire flowed through her, and she felt herself being pressed back into the pillow with a tender passion that cried of restraint.

Craig pulled away, breathless. His eyes steadied on hers. "I don't understand what's happening between us, but I think we need to explore it."

"Now?" she asked hopefully, all her reservations about this man forgotten in the need that flowed through her.

Oh, yes. He wanted to act on his need for her so badly he ached. But that wasn't why he'd brought her here. She was too vulnerable, too fragile at the moment. "No. Not tonight." He stood. "But soon."

"Craig." She caught his wrist. "No one can get in?"

"Don't worry. The security is great. That's why I brought you here."

"The Purity?"

"It's safe too. Look, we'll talk about all that tomorrow. When you're feeling better."

"Okay." She nodded, then winced in pain. "Oh, one more thing. The faux." Even knowing she might be pushing his generosity over the limit, she asked, "You'll let me make another, for Grandy?"

He sighed. "I'll think about it."

He split the next few hours between checking on Lyssa and considering her request to make another faux Purity. By bringing the necklace to her grandmother's deathbed in Arizona, he'd meant to help, but as it turned out, he'd only put Lyssa between a rock and a hard place.

He didn't like the idea of another copy; the one she'd already made had served only to put the real Purity in jeopardy. On the other hand, he couldn't shake from his mind the picture of Idella De-Haviland, her blue eyes aglow as they gazed at the necklace, her features softened as she thought of the happiness she expected the wedding necklace to bring to her granddaughter.

After one last check on Lyssa, he settled for the night on his living room sofa and closed his eyes, wishing he could come up with some solution that would satisfy them both.

Saturday

LYSSA WAS UP BEFORE CRAIG. She made coffee, showered, and dressed in the same suit she'd worn yesterday, the teal fabric smudged with dirt and spattered with dark stains. Blood, most likely. But she looked better, felt stronger and sounded like her old self.

Even the pain in her head and her ankle was tolerable. As Craig joined her in the kitchen, she said, "I have to be at the hotel in a half hour."

He yawned and stretched. "I thought maybe you'd want to skip that."

"I can't. Oh, I could get out of the speech, but that's not the point. If I run now, I'll always be looking over my shoulder, always living in fear, always behind locked doors. Like a caged animal. I can't let someone do that to me."

"If we just knew who."

"But we don't."

Craig washed down the lump in his throat with a swallow of coffee. He hadn't mentioned his suspicions about David and Stacey to her, but David had left a message on his answering machine yesterday, and as soon as Lyssa was at the convention, Craig intended to get some answers from both his cousin and David Lundeen.

She touched his whisker-bristled cheek and smiled softly. "Don't worry about me. I promise, I'll take precautions."

He didn't like it, but he knew if he were in her position, he'd carry on with his plans, too. "I'll be ready in ten minutes."

Craig showered, shaved and dressed in jeans and a white dress shirt. When he returned to the kitchen, Lyssa was standing where he'd left her, holding a cup of coffee and staring out at his view of the Space Needle.

She wheeled around, an anxious expression on her face. "I just called Grandy. Are you going to let me make another faux Purity?"

"I haven't decided yet." He had made a decision, but he would tell her about it only after he'd ascertained his plan was feasible and he'd worked out all the glitches. No sense getting her hopes up for nothing. "I'll let you know later today. How is your grandmother?"

"She's having a bad day," Lyssa snapped, frustrated and angry at whoever had her faux. Grandy's will to live was so fragile. The Purity had made her fight. The thought of attending Lyssa's wedding had given her something to live for. But without the Purity...she pressed her lips together. At least Craig hadn't said no. She'd have her answer sometime today. But could she make another faux Purity in time for Grandy?

Neither spoke on the drive to the Four Seasons. For all the reassurances she'd given Craig about not wanting to live in fear, Lyssa found herself glancing askance at every car, at every pedestrian. Craig went up to her room with her, made certain no one was hiding anywhere, then prepared to leave, kissing her gently. "What time will you be done today?"

"Around five, I think."

"I'll be here at six. If I get delayed, I'll leave you a message at the front desk."

BY FOUR-THIRTY, LYSSA was at the front desk checking for messages. The clerk said, "You have one from a Mr. C. Rival. Came in about half an hour ago."

Lyssa moved away from the counter and read the message. *I've found the faux. Meet me at Windance. Take all precautions. Don't tell anyone. Make sure no one follows. Craig.*

Her heart was pumping like a piston by the time she got to her room. Could it be? Could it really be? Would she have the faux Purity to take home to Grandy tomorrow night? Hope was straining at the bit inside her. She read the note again. The words *Take all precautions* seemed to leap out at her. Was this message really from Craig? How could she know for sure?

She called his condo and got the answering machine. Hanging up, she phoned his office, then Windance. Nothing. He must already be on his way. She dialed his car-phone number. After three rings she got another answering machine. Anxious frustration tightened her fingers on the receiver. He was probably in the car and the car was in an area unreachable by phone.

Maybe he'd call one of his machines. She left message that she was on her way and he should expect her at Windance around six-thirty or seven. She called Craig's condo again and left the same message

Twenty minutes later, she was climbing into a rental car, her blond hair hidden beneath a soft hat and her eyes behind large sunglasses. She paid particular attention to the rearview mirror. No one followed.

Traveling the North Shore Road alone caused a few frightening flashbacks, but by dusk she arrived at Windance unscathed. The gate was open. Lights were on inside the house. Lyssa spotted Craig's Lexus and breathed a sigh of relief. He was here. By tomorrow night she'd be on a plane, headed home with the faux. Finally something was going right.

She hurried across the porch. But when she knocked, he didn't answer. She tried the door. It was unlocked. "Craig?"

She stepped into the foyer and locked the door. "Craig!"

The scent of fresh coffee drew her into the kitchen. There she found a note and a mug next to the coffee-maker. *Gone next door. Be back before you finish the cup.* Smiling, Lyssa filled the mug, then carried it to the table and settled her coat over a chair.

The phone rang.

It startled her, and she realized she was not all that comfortable being alone in this house. She snatched up the receiver on the second ring. "Hello?"

"Lyssa, thank God!"

"Craig?"

"Are you all right?"

"Of course."

"Why did you go to Windance?"

A shudder ran through her. "Your message. You said you found the faux."

"I didn't send you any message."

"What?" Cold fear flooded her stomach as Lyssa stared out the window at Craig's Lexus. "Where are you?"

"In Seattle. Someone stole my car."

Chapter Twelve

"It's here," Lyssa whispered, terror gripping her so fiercely she felt as if she were strangling. "The Lexus is here."

"Get out of there!" Craig shouted.

Lyssa dropped the receiver and ran to her coat, digging in the pocket for the key to her car. Footsteps. Coming from the living room. Panic shot through her. She spun toward the doorway leading to the foyer. Shadows fell across the walls. She couldn't breathe.

The beach. It was her only hope. She wheeled around and sped out the kitchen door and across the deck. The slivered moon cast eerie pools of light on the dark waters of the canal. She ran for the seawall stairs and stepped down. Icy water saturated her foot, her pant leg. The tide was in. She was trapped.

Footsteps sounded on the deck behind her. Lyssa pulled her foot from the water and whirled around.

Out of the shadows near the gaping door, a dark blur raced at her.

Shrieking, Lyssa reared back, lost her balance and landed hard on her fanny, knocking the wind out of herself.

The person was on her in an instant, clamping a gloved hand over her mouth and shoving her head toward the water. Terror roared through her veins, and Lyssa fought like a wild woman. But too much had happened to her in the past few days. Within seconds, her strength was spent. She felt as weak as a baby. The attacker plunged her head under the water.

The pressure on Lyssa's face felt like the weight of death. Her fists flailed impotently against her attacker's arms. Her skull pounded with pain. Her lungs burned. Horrified, Lyssa realized she would soon give in to her craving for breath.

And die.

CRAIG'S HEART WAS in his throat. He abandoned his rental car before it came to a complete stop, and he sprinted through the gate at Windance. Had the police arrived too late? He ran up the drive, took the porch steps two at a time and skidded into the foyer.

Voices sounded in the kitchen. Every breath hurt as he plunged headlong into the room. Then he spotted her, sitting at the table, talking quietly to Officer Kaslow. Craig almost collapsed with relief. "Lyssa."

"Craig?" Her head jerked up and she leapt from the chair and into his open arms. She clung to him as she had that first day, her arms wrapped around his waist, her head burrowed against his chest. Her hair hung loose, smelling as if she'd recently showered. She trembled like a frightened bird, and he had an awful sense of déjà vu. This nightmare was far from over.

"We figure our sirens scared him off," Officer Kaslow said, rising from the table.

"It was a man, then?"

The policewoman shrugged and left the room.

Lyssa shook her head. "I don't know. I couldn't tell. It was dark and I—"

"It's all right. I understand." Craig led her back to the table and soon handed her a brandy-laced cup of coffee. He sat next to her, and Lyssa grasped his hand, then told him of her ordeal.

Craig listened with impotent rage, glancing away from her only when his old friend Sgt. Bob Archer entered the room. Bob, a born-again bachelor, as he liked to call himself since his divorce five years earlier, was the handsomest man Craig knew. He wore his ash blond hair cropped close, favored a trim mustache and short sideburns, and sported a perpetual tan.

They exchanged greetings.

"We found the Lexus three doors up," Bob said. "But no trace of the perp. We're doing a house-by-house."

Craig pressed his lips in a flat line and nodded grimly.

Bob joined them at the table. "I don't have the manpower to guard you two. I think you should get the hell out of here. Head back to Seattle."

Lyssa's eyes widened at the suggestion. "Will I be any safer there?"

At Bob's querulous expression, Craig filled him in on all that had been happening, including their theories about the Purity and the faux, the hit-and-run accident and their fear that Lyssa had been the actual target.

"Agreed. I'm not a believer in coincidence." Bob tilted his head toward Lyssa. "You have any theories as to why this person wants you dead?"

She glanced uneasily at Craig, then back at Bob. "Craig believes whoever it is thinks I've figured out their identity."

Bob considered that a minute. "Yeah, but that doesn't explain the first attack on you."

He had a point, Craig realized, and it concurred with something he'd wondered about before. "Could there be two people after her?"

"Seems unlikely, but stranger things have happened. You have any likely suspects?"

Craig knew he should tell him about David and Stacey, but he wanted first to tell Lyssa. "Not really."

"Well, if you think of someone, let me know. I'm going to check my radio, see if we're making any progress." He shoved back his chair and strode into the foyer.

"You do suspect someone," Lyssa said the second Craig and she were alone. "Who?"

He watched her sip from the cup, could see that the brandy was taking the edge off her shock. "I have no proof, but where the copy and the Purity are concerned, I have to admit that you're right about Stacey and David both having had the opportunity to take the necklaces from here, and to return the Purity to the office vault in Seattle. Plus, David is the most likely Lundeen to have drawn up your agreement with Wayne. After all, he's handled all of the company's business since his third year out of law school. And Stacey and he seem to have gotten close while I was in Europe. Of course, they both deny it."

"You actually accused them?" The coffee cup wobbled in her hand.

"Not accused, exactly. I spoke to David first. Then drove to Stacey's. They both took exception to my questions and were both adamant they knew nothing of the faux Purity. It was while I was at Stacey's in West Seattle that the Lexus was stolen. David could have taken it. He knew I'd be at Stacey's and he knows where I keep a key."

Lyssa could see the torment that thinking along these lines caused him. She'd had a few unpleasant thoughts of her own. "What about my cousin Ginger?"

Craig frowned. "What about her?"

"She was awfully upset at Wayne's funeral. If you were sincere about your uncle's taste in women, she certainly fits the bill. Suppose she cozied up to Wayne and he told her about the copy? There's certainly no love lost between us. She could have had the opportunity to take the necklaces." Not to mention motive galore, if she was still involved with Kevin. He was always embroiled in some get-rich-quick scheme or another.

A wayward thought struck Craig. "Or C.J. Temple."

"C.J.?"

"Yesterday, she offered me a king's ransom for the Purity."

This news stunned Lyssa. Why hadn't Teri told her? "Why would C.J. offer to buy the necklace, if she planned on stealing it?"

"To cast suspicion elsewhere?"

"I hate thinking someone I know is trying to kill me." Lyssa took a long swallow of spiked coffee. But what if misplaced loyalty resulted in her death? She shuddered. Something Sergeant Archer had said came back to her. There had to be a reason for all the attacks on her, even the first one. Had she inadvertently seen something that somehow threatened the stalker? Did she know something she didn't know she knew, something the killer was afraid she would recall? She straightened, lifting her head. Of course. That had to be it.

She told Craig. "Now, if I could figure out whatever it is..." She closed her eyes and racked her brain, but nothing popped to mind.

"You'll remember," Craig encouraged her, tracing her cheek with his hand.

But would she live long enough to remember? Lyssa wondered.

IT WAS NEAR ELEVEN when Bob Archer returned. He shook his head at Craig's unasked question and sighed. "You two look pretty done in. Mind if I make a suggestion?"

"What?"

"I don't think any of the local motels are going to inspire you with feelings of security, and there are a lot of back roads that aren't particularly safe this time of night." Bob combed his mustache with the edge of his index finger. "Why don't you stay the night at my place? Always a bottle of wine and a couple of thawed steaks in the fridge. I'll bunk with a lady friend in town and no one will be the wiser."

Craig looked at Lyssa. "What do you think?"

She nodded. "Thank you, Sergeant."

"You're welcome. Meanwhile, I'm taking the Lexus into the lab for a thorough going-over. Should be ready in the morning."

They devised a plan to get them out of Windance as anonymously as possible. Then, as Lyssa carried her cup to the sink, Craig followed Bob into the foyer, exchanging house and car keys.

"I don't expect the car will yield much—a few fibers, maybe a hair if we're lucky."

Craig filled him in on their list of suspects.

"I'll call someone I know on the Seattle PD and pass this on to him. He'll be in touch."

"I owe you big-time."

"No problem." Bob started past him, then stopped. "Oh, incidentally, Cannibal is loose."

CLOAK-AND-DAGGER had always sounded like fun. Reality left a lot to be desired, Lyssa reflected, lying flat on the back seat of Bob Archer's unmarked Ford, wishing her heart would soothe its erratic beat. She gripped the handle of her purse, reassured by the gun inside it that Craig had insisted she borrow for protection.

As much as she disliked these precautions, she believed they were necessary. Officer Kaslow had left in her car, dressed in her clothes, with the braid she favored brushed loose in a simulation of her hairstyle.

The stalker could be anywhere. Cold sweat broke over her body.

Bob Archer would be the last to leave Windance. Half an hour from now, dressed like Craig, he would lock the gates and drive the Lexus into town to the police lab.

Lyssa closed her eyes. What was it that she knew? Who was doing this to her? She felt like screaming. Instead, she opened her eyes and stared at the interior of the car's roof, the pressing darkness relieved only by the dull gleam of dashboard lights. "Are we being followed?"

"Not so far," Craig answered. "But don't get up until I tell you. We're at Bob's driveway now." The tension in his voice echoed the tension zipping along her veins.

The car took a sudden sharp left, then ascended, bouncing up a rutted road. Pressed against the back of the seat, Lyssa strained to hear, fearing that at any second the crunch of tires on the gravel behind them would shatter her fragile sense of security. That the revolver would be needed.

A second later, Craig parked and turned off the engine. He opened his door, whispering, "Don't get out of the car."

Lyssa heard the gentle clicking as he closed the door, heard his muffled footsteps as he raced behind the car and presumably down the road they'd just come up. Then all was quiet. Too quiet. She waited a minute. Two. Three. Four. Had something happened to him? She could almost feel the air inside the car dissipating. Why couldn't she pinpoint the memory that could solve this for her? Sweat pooled on her upper lip. What if the stalker found her cowering in this car? She was a sitting duck. At least outside she'd have a fighting chance.

She opened her door as quietly as Craig had closed his. Clutching her purse against her, she left the car. The night air was chilly on her clammy skin.

The Ford was parked before an A-frame cabin that was centered on about a quarter acre of cleared land. Behind it, the forest was dense on the mountainside. In front, the view was incredible—the sprinkling of home and business lights twinkling against the darkness as if for her pleasure. It gave her none.

The stalker was out there somewhere . . . waiting for her. Maybe coming up the driveway even now.

Panic blossomed inside Lyssa. Where was Craig? He'd been gone well over five minutes. She jammed her hand into her purse and withdrew the pistol. Just in case. She scrutinized the moonlit driveway, seeking his familiar form, dreading seeing that other form.

A low growling brought her jerking around. Her heart crawled into her throat. A huge black mastiff was advancing on her, its teeth bared. Lyssa gulped. Her racing heart seemed to stop altogether. "Nice doggie."

Another growl.

"I'm friend, not foe." She stuck a shaking hand toward him, praying he wouldn't snap it off with those fearsome fangs. Any sudden moves, even a dash for her open car door, might spur an attack. She gripped the gun tighter. "Nice doggie."

His breath fogged the cool air as he gained on her.

Horrified at the thought, but realizing it might be her only option, she said, "Don't make me shoot you, fella."

"Cannibal!" Craig's voice cut through the tension, catching both the dog and Lyssa by surprise.

Cannibal glanced from one to the other, his ears twitching. Craig approached, talking to him all the while in gentle tones.

Somehow Lyssa's legs held her upright. Her body was as rigid as one of the pines behind the cabin. Three feet from the dog, Craig knelt, offering his hand for Cannibal to catch his scent. She held her breath. The mastiff took his time deciding. Then his stance slackened slightly and he retracted his teeth. Craig let out an audible sigh.

Relief rolled through Lyssa. Craig glanced over his shoulder. "What are you doing out here? I told you to wait in the car."

"You were gone so long—"

"I was listening to see if anyone came up the drive."

"And?"

"Nothing." He had his hand on the dog's collar. "Now, come here, slowly. Cannibal's not a pet, but once he knows you're a friend, he won't harm you."

Lyssa shoved the gun into her purse, and with stiff, measured steps, walked toward them. Craig reached for her hand, and she clutched his as if it were a lifeline. A moment later, Cannibal sniffed her hand. Lyssa couldn't stop trembling.

Craig rose. "At night or whenever Bob is away, Cannibal patrols the perimeters. We'll be as safe as if we were in jail. Safer."

"It's not the dog. It's—" It was everything. The whole ordeal. Grandy. The stalker. The hit-and-run accident. Tonight. All of it crashing down on her.

Releasing her hand, he drew her into his arms. "It's all right."

Was it? Would anything ever be all right again? She curled against his chest, feeling the first sense of reassurance in hours, feeling protected, sheltered. She hadn't trusted any man in three years. Since Kevin's betrayal. But she trusted Craig Rival. With her heart. With her very life.

He led her to the door and deactivated Bob's security system, reactivating it as soon as they were inside and had turned on a few lights. Eucalyptus scented the air. The cabin was small, clean and open. An eating counter, shaped like a *J,* was the only division between living room and kitchen.

Lyssa noticed a spiral staircase leading to the loft that served as the second floor, and likely Bob's bedroom. The police sergeant seemed fond of red, white and blue, and the combination gave his home a cheery, masculine appeal.

"Why don't you sit down?" Craig gestured toward the navy leather sofa.

As she complied, he began filling the fireplace with kindling. "A nice fire will take the chill off this place."

And he was right. Within the hour, she had ceased trembling, had realized how hungry she was and joined him in preparing steaks, potatoes and a salad.

Now they sat close together on the sofa, plates on their laps, the fire crackling, soft music on the stereo. "More wine?" Craig asked.

She extended her glass, appreciating that he hadn't mentioned the attacks on her. Dwelling on that another moment tonight would strip the fragile layers of her composure. She needed this normalcy, this reaffirmation of life, as she'd never needed it before in all her twenty-eight years. She sipped her wine, then asked, "Why is it you've never married?"

Craig studied her face. She was calmer than he'd seen her in hours. And here, at least, was a subject he could talk about. "My parents had one of those wonderful marriages most people dream about but seldom accomplish." He gave her a wry grin. "I'm not willing to settle for less. And so far, most of the women I've been serious about cared more about what I could give them than they cared about me."

Lyssa knew women like that. "Well, I don't care to ever try marriage again."

"Pretty bad experience, huh?"

"The worst. Try finding your mate in bed with your sexy cousin."

So *that* explained her hostility toward Ginger Van Allen. He grimaced. "Ouch!"

Lyssa nodded. "I thought Kevin loved me. Now I realize he's incapable of really loving anyone. He's stingy and selfish, a real egomaniac." Then again, what could she have expected from an insecure man who made his living by his looks? Probably all male models weren't as vain as Kevin, but she supposed it *was* a hazard of their profession, what with everyone always telling them how wonderful they looked. A clamminess swept her skin. Shakily, she lifted her wineglass and sipped. Thoughts of Kevin always upset her, and she didn't want to be upset. Not tonight. Talk about something else. "You know the De-Haviland history—why Mom and Grandy want the Purity back in my family—but none of us know why it's so important to you."

Now it was Craig's turn to face difficult memories. "As you know, the necklace was created as a wedding gift, as a symbol of the purity of the groom's love for his bride."

"My great-great-grandfather and -grandmother."

Craig nodded. "As per tradition, Dad gave Mom the necklace on their wedding day. She treasured it, as she did him." A tender gleam came into his dark eyes. "She used to look at it the same way your grandmother looked at it, as if it had some magical power. My mother's dying wish was that I give it to my bride, the daughter-in-law she would never know."

Lyssa felt a catch in her chest. She'd once wondered if family meant as much to him as it did to her. Obviously it did. His mother sounded like someone she'd liked to have known, and at long last she understood his possessiveness of the Purity—could, indeed, relate to it.

She watched him walk across the room to the stereo. The wine was making her languid. She stretched her legs onto the coffee table as if this were her own home. She was comfortable here with Craig. Something about him relaxed her. Maybe it was his upbringing. She envied him growing up in a harmonious environment.

Michael Bolton's soulful voice, eschewing the virtues of loving, issued from the speakers. Lyssa sighed. Her parents' idea of loving was screaming . . . about everything. Wincing at the memories, she swallowed more wine. She doubted very much—as Grandy seemed to think—whether the Purity would have smoothed the rough waters of their matrimonial sea.

The DeHavilands hadn't helped, either, siding with her mother after every quarrel, until Roxanne's loyalties shredded and her marriage collapsed. The sad truth was, although they still loved one another, her parents simply couldn't live together.

Given that and her own experience, she thought Craig wise not marrying until he was certain. Marriage was such a gamble. You had to be willing to risk your heart and soul, give up your independence, and sometimes your individuality. A heavy price. And even then, outside influences could rip it apart.

She gathered the dishes, carried them to the sink and loaded the dishwasher as Craig wrapped the leftovers and cleaned the counter and grill. They were sharing the mundane tasks like any couple on an autumn night. Except that they weren't any couple, and this night hadn't been like any other night. She tensed. No, she would not think about it.

"All done?" As if he'd seen the slight tensing of her shoulders, Craig gripped her by the upper arms and gently pulled her around, then brought his deft fingers to her neck and massaged the taut muscles. His face was inches from hers, his warm breath fanning her lashes, her cheeks, her lips.

She gazed up into his dark, dark eyes, saw the smoldering light there and felt a jolting current of awareness course through her, that sudden flaring of desire that possessed her whenever he was near.

"Maybe this isn't the perfect time or place...." The huskiness in his voice intensified the sweet shivers streaming through her. "But you're leaving tomorrow and there may never be another moment for us. I want you, and I think you want me."

He wasn't asking for a commitment. No, this was something much simpler, much more basic, and it was something she was ready and willing to give.

"Oh, yes." A quavery breath rushed from her as his hands left her shoulders, skimmed down her arms, then up again, higher, higher, grazing the sensitive flesh of her neck, until they cupped her head, and he lowered his mouth to hers. The contact created an electrical energy, releasing need and hunger in equal measure, converting her bones to water, water that was slowly being heated to a roiling boil.

She heard herself murmur his name as she wrapped her arms around his neck, laced her fingers through his thick blue-black hair and arched her body against his. Craig carried her into the living room and laid her gently on the thick area rug that was spread before the fireplace.

Lyssa felt as if she were sinking into a sumptuous abyss. All that seemed to matter was this place, this man, this overpowering need to give and take. She had no memory of clothes disappearing, only of his glorious nakedness brushing hers. She surrendered to his touches, his kisses, the forays of his erotic tongue, and with her long hair whisking his belly like silken blond feathers, she bestowed and explored in like turns.

Then he was pulling her to him, his lips claiming hers as his body claimed hers, joining, uniting in the age-old way that felt as if they'd just invented it. Joy and passion rocked through her with every thrust, searing her as if she'd been burned by the fire, lifting her as if she were soaring toward the moon on wings of love. And then heaven and all its stars came tumbling down to meet her in a wild, giddy explosion as brilliant and breathtakingly beautiful as the grandest fireworks display.

Afterward, they lay in each other's arms, warmed by the fire, soothed by the dim lighting, lulled by the sensuous music and the slowing of their hearts.

Craig brushed a lock of hair from her face. Stripped of his condom, he wore only a wry grin. "You really are a witch."

"What?"

"An enchanting sorceress." And he was her willing captive. Instead of getting her out of his system, he wanted her all the more. She smiled up at him, and he reached for her again.

Sunday

AROUND TEN, BOB ARRIVED with the Lexus, which had been given a going-over by the Belmont police lab. "Picked up a few clues. I'll let you know if anything specific turns up on it."

Lyssa and Craig thanked him, then started for Seattle. Lyssa seemed calmer, as if their lovemaking had managed to restore her sense of well-being. She still hadn't remembered what she'd seen or what she knew that was putting her in jeopardy. Maybe he could help. "Why don't you tell me everything you can remember about that Monday, the last time you saw the copy and the Purity together?"

They spent the next hour examining her memories of that day, but as Seattle came into view, neither had come up with anything someone might consider threatening. Craig felt as if they were getting nowhere. One glance at Lyssa told him she was every bit as frustrated. He reached for her hand and changed the subject. "I never told you what I decided about the faux Purity."

Over the last twenty-four hours, Lyssa had come to a new realization about the copy. She stared at the traffic, seeing instead the disappointment that would soon be on Grandy's face. "Forget it. You were right. Perhaps the faux would have fooled Grandy last week, before she held the real one. But last week I hadn't considered I was making a mockery of her beliefs, and now I know that's exactly what the copy is. She deserves better from me."

As he exited the interstate, he said, "You tried to do something special for her. You wanted to grant her dying wish, and if it weren't for—" He bit off the words. So much for changing the subject.

They stopped at her hotel long enough for Lyssa to change clothes. Craig was wearing blue jeans, cowboy boots, a white cotton shirt and his black leather jacket. She changed clothes into something similarly comfortable, equally generic, and they were soon back in the Lexus, winding through the streets of Seattle toward Pike Place Market, the oldest continuously operated farmers' market in the United States.

She couldn't think of any place quite like it. Part of its appeal was that no chain stores or franchises were allowed; it was a small-business owner's haven. Lyssa needed to consult with one such merchant, and afterward Craig and she would enjoy a late lunch at Cutter's Bayhouse before he took her to the airport.

The crisp October day radiated sunshine. People were out in droves, meandering among the stalls and shops.

Lyssa, her nose twitching at the ripe odor of fresh fish, led Craig through the main arcade, past the famous bronze pig and down one flight of stairs to the first floor. Foot traffic here was less congested.

The store she sought was near the stairs and sold women's clothing. The owner, a disgruntled matron who didn't trust men, eyed Craig with suspicion. Lyssa suggested he window-shop until she finished.

Her business took almost an hour longer than she'd expected. Through the shop window, she spotted Craig out in the main walkway. She headed for the door, but when she got outside, Craig had moved away. Foot traffic had grown denser. She scanned the crowd. Some distance away, near the stairs, she spied his dark hair, his black leather jacket.

His back was to her, and he was too far away to hear her call his name unless she shouted. She started after him. He turned his head from side to side, as though something had his attention. Something down the stairwell. As if to confirm this, he started down the stairs.

Pressing her shoulder bag—the gun tucked inside—tight against her hip, she hurried after him as fast as her sore ankle allowed. She reached the landing and peered into the stairwell. There he was, dipping just out of sight. "Craig!"

The only answer was the echo of his retreating footfalls. Cautiously, Lyssa descended. Down one level, then another, into the bowels of the market. No longer could she hear the reassuring chatter of people.

Her pulse thrummed unpleasantly. She reached the last step, and there he was, his back to her. "Craig?"

He spun around. Her heart crawled into her throat. It wasn't Craig. But she knew those pale green eyes and knew before he tugged the black wig from his head that this was the person who'd been trying to kill her. "Kevin?" Her throat constricted. "Why?"

Her ex-husband's cover-boy-handsome face grew ugly with hatred and rage as he leapt at her, brandishing a switchblade inches from her face. Lyssa lurched back, swinging wildly with her purse. The shoulder bag nailed his wrist.

The knife flew loose, clattering down another flight of stairs, followed by her purse—with Craig's gun still nestled inside. She whirled away from him and dived for the stairs.

Roaring wildly, Kevin was on her in a flash, grasping her from behind, his hands encircling her throat.

Chapter Thirteen

Kevin's thumbs pressed into Lyssa's windpipe, cutting off her scream. She kicked back ineffectually, tore at his hands with her own, tried twisting free. But he was too strong. Points of light danced before her eyes, and pain circled her throat as he dragged her away from the stairs.

Lyssa smelled his sour breath, which mingled with the murky odor of his perfumed after-shave and her own salty fear. Kevin's mouth was against her ear. "Why couldn't you just stay out of my life?"

She had no idea what he was ranting about, couldn't answer him even if she had. The pressure behind her eyes increased. Her temples throbbed. He swung her around his hip as he might a Frisbee before sailing it through the air, and she realized with cold terror that he meant to hurl her down the steps onto the concrete embankment below.

Adrenaline spurted through Lyssa. With the strength of her will to live, she punched backward, ramming her fist into his groin. He let out a startled yelp and released her. Lyssa, dizzy from lack of oxygen, staggered to the edge of the landing.

A loud, outraged roar snapped her gaze into focus. Head bent, Kevin was charging her like an irate bull. She commanded her body to move, but her limbs froze.

Then somehow, miraculously, Craig and Teri were there, running down the stairs, calling to them.

Craig leapt from the upper staircase into Kevin's path. Kevin hopped to avoid being tackled, but Craig clipped him on the ankle, catapulting him straight at Lyssa.

Teri screamed.

Lyssa ducked.

Kevin, a look of sheer surprise on his face, sailed off the landing, his body cracking against the concrete as he tumbled down the stairs.

"Lyssa!" Craig caught her against him.

Teri raced down the steps after Kevin, then shouted up to them, "He's alive, but his pulse is weak. Call an ambulance."

Craig sat Lyssa down on a step, then rushed for help.

For Lyssa, the next hour was a whirl of medical and law enforcement tumult. After Kevin was hustled to the hospital, a police officer in tow who would read him his rights and take his statement the moment he regained consciousness, Teri, Craig and Lyssa settled in a corner at Cutter's Bayhouse, sipping straight brandy and shaking off the aftershocks of the ordeal.

Craig had suggested taking Lyssa immediately to his condo, but she'd needed the reassurance of seeing strangers occupied in ordinary activities. And she'd needed to talk about what had happened, with people who seemed to care about her. "I thought I was a goner. How did you two find me?"

Teri glanced at Craig, obviously still uncertain that this was the best place for Lyssa after what she'd been through. "I was coming down from the main arcade when I spotted you—although at the time I thought it was just someone who looked like you—starting down to the next level. A minute later I ran into Craig. He asked if I'd seen you anywhere, and we decided to investigate."

"It's a good thing we did." Craig reached for Lyssa's hand, but she casually drew it out of his reach, as if she couldn't stand being touched, as if she were suddenly unsure of her feelings for him. Was she? Had Kevin made that much of a difference? Or was she regretting their night of passion?

"I thought I knew Kevin." Teri shuddered, and Lyssa wondered again how close she and Kevin might have become. Teri swirled her drink absently. "It's so bizarre...his trying to kill you."

"I'm just glad the nightmare is over." Glad the stalker was caught. Lyssa didn't want to dwell on the attacks; she knew they would haunt her dreams in the nights ahead, but at least she could go about her life without being in constant fear. The brandy was making her sleepy, and eventually she gave in to Craig's insistence that the two of them retreat to his condo to await the police officer Bob Archer had contacted. He'd promised to let them know what the search of Kevin's apartment yielded.

It was a good three hours later before he showed up at the condo. Detective Jackson, a stocky black man in his midforties, had with him the photograph missing from Craig's wallet, Lyssa's wristwatch and a key, all of which had been found in the pocket of an overcoat in Kevin's closet.

The key hadn't fit anything in Kevin's apartment, and Jackson wanted to know if it looked familiar to Craig or Lyssa. After comparing it with their own keys, they discovered it matched the front-door key to Windance.

"I'd say that ties the package neat and tidy then," Jackson said, pocketing the key and the photograph.

"What do you suppose he wanted with that snapshot?" Craig asked.

"You said you'd never met him before. The way he's circled your face in red, I'd guess he took it to identify you."

That sounded plausible enough, Craig decided. "Didn't you find the faux Purity?"

"Nope. Figure he's got that stashed someplace for safe keeping."

Craig nodded. "How is he doing?"

Jackson shook his head. "The hospital's listed him in critical condition. His worst injury is a broken neck. From my understanding, if he survives the night, he'll likely live, but he might not walk again."

Craig felt no pity for Kevin. The man had set upon a murderous course and now would pay the piper. He saw the detective out and returned to Lyssa.

She looked dwarfed on his deep-cushioned leather couch, as if all she'd undergone had sucked away a part of her, rendering her smaller than before. But she was safe at last, and soon her inner strength would rekindle, burning bright and clear, and she would put all this behind her. His heart thumped. Would she put *him* behind her, too?

The idea rattled him to his toes, forcing Craig to look anew at his feelings for Lyssa. Was it possible to fall in love with someone in ten days? He swallowed a laugh. Whether or not it was possible didn't really matter. He *had* fallen in love with her.

He hadn't the faintest idea where it would lead. Her poor opinion of marriage was born of personal experience. And, after just having it confirmed that her ex-husband had been trying to kill her, it was likely she'd never take the plunge again. He remembered how she'd flinched when he'd tried to take her hand at the restaurant. *Damn Kevin Carlyle!* Why had he done it? Craig sank to the couch beside her, but made no move to touch her. Not until she was ready. "Why?"

She didn't need to ask what he was talking about. She knew. She'd been sitting there thinking, going over that Monday night again, and suddenly she stiffened. "Oh, my God. I remember. I was driving away from Windance, hadn't gone more than a few yards, when my purse fell over. I glanced down as I righted it, and when I looked up, I realized I was on a collision course with a car parked just beyond the fence. I avoided the crash by inches, but I noticed a man sitting in the car and thought he reminded me of someone. A couple miles down the road, I was thinking about something else, and I haven't thought of it since, until now."

"It was Kevin in the car?"

"Yes." She nodded, still frowning. "What was he doing at Windance minutes before Wayne died?"

"Could he have known Wayne?"

"It's more likely that Wayne told Ginger about the copy I was making and that she told Kevin."

"He didn't follow you that night, or visit the house while you were still there?"

"No."

"Then what happened later to worry him that you could place him at Windance at that particular time?"

She considered a moment. "The faux Purity was stolen."

Craig nodded. "Maybe Kevin found Wayne dead, then discovered the necklaces."

"Maybe he knew the necklaces would be there and came with the intention of stealing them, but after he thought I'd seen him, he opted for another plan, fearing I'd point the finger at him."

"But if Wayne wasn't involved, how did Kevin expect to—?" Craig felt as if he'd been struck with a stick. He scowled at the natural progression of his thoughts, at the prickling against the base of his skull. "Do you suppose Kevin murdered Wayne?"

They stared at one another, digesting this. The thought of Wayne being murdered staggered Craig. Angered him. But the more he considered it, the less outlandish it seemed.

At length, Lyssa said, "I wouldn't have believed such a thing yesterday, but today... Was an autopsy performed?"

"Wayne's bad heart was common knowledge." He rose and paced the length of the room. "I doubt anything else was even considered."

Lyssa pulled her knees to her chin. "And now it's too late to find out for sure."

"Is it?" He hustled to the telephone and dialed David. When Craig identified himself, David's reception was cool. Craig wasted no time apologizing for his behavior of the day before, and was glad that David seemed placated. He updated him on recent events and confided his suspicions about Wayne's death, asking the legalities of what he wanted arranged.

"It isn't easy to get an exhumation order," David told him. "You'll need Stacey to agree to it. Without her consent it will be nearly impossible."

Stacey was still bristling about Craig's treatment of her the day before. His apology did not placate her. Indeed, his request seemed to ice the cake. "You have a lot of nerve."

Craig wondered what he had expected. First, he had all but accused her of attacking Lyssa, and now he wanted to dig up her father's body. "Please reconsider. I think it's very likely Kevin Carlyle killed your father. We owe it to Wayne to prove it."

A shuddered breath rushed down the line and into his ear. "It's too gruesome. I won't have Dad disturbed in order to indulge your see-it-for-yourself fixation."

There was no use persisting tonight. She wasn't about to consider anything he said. But maybe when she'd had time to think. He rang off and hung up. "She refuses to cooperate."

"Well, that's that, then."

"Maybe not." Craig ran his hands through his hair. "David said it would be *nearly* impossible."

Just then, the telephone rang.

It was Detective Jackson. "Kevin Carlyle is conscious and asking for Ms. Carlyle."

Too bad. Craig tamped down the anger that flashed inside him at the thought of Lyssa having to face that maniac again. But it was her decision, not his. He thanked the detective and replaced the receiver, turning gingerly toward her. Her eager expression gave him pause.

"What?" She half rose from the couch. "Has something happened I should know about? Craig...?"

Craig relayed the message. "You don't have to go."

Lyssa sank again onto the thick cushions. Her expression shifted from disbelief to disgust to determination; a light bounced in her beautiful eyes, the first he'd seen in hours. She hopped off the sofa. "I want to see him. It's important that I defuse his power over me." She gathered her coat and purse. "And, if I'm lucky, maybe I can get the answers we want and Wayne won't need to be disturbed."

"Don't do this on that account."

"I told you, I'm doing this for me." Lyssa was surprised at how strong she felt. Just having her stalker identified and stopped had purged most of her fear. Confronting Kevin would rid her of the rest.

HARBORVIEW, THE COUNTY trauma center, was unlike any hospital Lyssa had encountered. The ambulance traffic was copious, their sirens grating on her nerves, and the heavy beat of rotor blades as airlift helicopters arrived or departed was more jarring still. These noises merged with the general commotion of people moving through the halls, the buzz of conversations and the disembodied voice on the intercom system paging doctors. There was a sense of life and death, a sense of immediacy, a more earthy environment than the tidy clinic atmosphere of most hospitals.

She was allowed five minutes alone with Kevin. Craig promised to wait right outside the room. His concern was evident in the fierce tilt of his dark brows.

Her heart thundered as she turned her back on the man who'd saved her life and proceeded into the room to face the man who'd done his best to end it.

Kevin lay helpless, protracted on a circle bed. What looked to Lyssa like giant tongs protruded from his skull, as if his head were a planet surrounded by metal rings. A soft hissing emanated from the oxygen supplied to him through nasal prongs, and a steady beeping issued from a cardiac monitor.

Despite everything, she felt a flicker of pity for him. But not enough to ever forgive what he'd tried to do to her. Only sheer force of will brought her to the head of the bed, gave her the strength to stare at his bruised face, meet his pale icy eyes. "Why, Kevin? What did I ever do to you?"

A derisive laugh died in his throat, the effort obviously paining him. "Why?"

"Yes, why? You owe me an explanation and I want it."

"Always the smug, superior witch, aren't you?"

Lyssa drew in a breath of pungent antiseptic smells, then sighed. Same old song and dance. Was this worth putting herself through? She turned to leave.

"Listen."

She spun around. "Not to this garbage. If that's all you want, I'm out the door."

"Not all I want to say." His eyes looked angry and the monitored beeping increased with every word. "You always ruin things for me."

"*Me* ruining things for you?" Lyssa snapped. "I've stayed out of your life."

"Not true. I know you got . . . your dad to spoil my deal with Savage Cologne . . .'cause Ginger couldn't stay out of my bed." The beeps leapt faster, the rhythm irregular. "Savage was going to make me a...superstar!"

"If you lost the contract with Savage Cologne, it was your own doing. I never asked Dad to use his influence with Michael Savage one way or the other on your behalf. You got the job on your own, and I presume you lost it the same way. I didn't care what happened to you after—" She clamped her mouth shut. He knew after what.

Kevin acted as if he hadn't heard her. "Ha! I figured out how...to pay DeHavilands back. Their precious Purity lost forever." He closed his eyes and swallowed hard. The graphics on the monitor screen danced crazily. Then his cold gaze was on her. "You...ruined it. You saw me."

So, they'd been right. He hadn't wanted it known he'd been at Craig's house that night. Her pulse skittered. "What were you doing at Windance?"

"Wayne was backing out of our deal to steal... Purity. He was going to destroy the copy. Wouldn't listen to reason. Left me no choice. Couldn't let him ruin *this* deal. Not him. Not you." A glazed look came over his eyes, and his voice took on a singsong tone, as if he were talking to himself. As if he wasn't actually aware that Lyssa was there. The beeping sounded less frantic. "But you wouldn't die as...easy as Wayne."

A layer of ice spread through her stomach. He had killed Wayne, but how was Craig going to take the rest of the news? Kevin had had a partner all right. Not Ginger, but Wayne. She clenched her hands tighter together. "How did Wayne die? How did you murder him?"

She held her breath, waiting.

Kevin's eyes were closed again. She realized the monitor had reverted to a steady, regular rhythm, and heard now his even breathing. "Kevin?"

The door swung open and the nurse entered. She went directly to Kevin and checked his pulse and the monitor. "You'll have to leave."

"But I—"

"He's asleep," the nurse said. "The medication, you know."

"HE CONFESSED," she told Craig the moment she joined him in the hallway. "But he fell asleep before I could get him to tell me how he killed Wayne."

Craig swore. "Did he tell you why?"

How could she soften the blow? She could think of nothing that would make what she had to say any easier for him to hear. Recounting her discussion with Kevin as accurately as memory allowed, Lyssa told him of Wayne's part in the plan to steal the Purity.

He looked dumbstruck and betrayed. She led him to a bench and made him sit. After a moment, Craig said, "I was always fond of Wayne. Always felt a little sorry for him. My grandparents adopted him after being told they couldn't have children of their own. A year later my father, Paul, was born. It was obvious, even to me, that Granddad, Channing Rival, didn't love Wayne the way he loved Dad. He treated him as though he were a disappointment at every turn. The harder Wayne tried, the bigger he failed."

Lyssa nodded and took his hand.

Craig was quiet a moment, staring at the traffic in the busy hospital hall. "Worse still, Granddad instilled his prejudice for Wayne in Dad, and my father came to think of his brother as inferior. How that must have hurt Wayne." He leaned his head against the wall. "I remember once seeing a look of pure hatred in his eyes after Dad dressed him down in front of Stacey and me for selling a pendant to a longtime customer for a hundred dollars less than the sticker price. It was absurd. Dad would have done the same for this particular customer."

Pity for Wayne wound around Lyssa's heart. She didn't approve of what he'd done, but she could understand the years of frustration and impotency that had probably led him to the point of wanting to strike back at the Rivals.

"Why didn't Dad see what damage he was doing to his brother's spirit? Didn't he care?" Craig asked so quietly she had to lean closer to hear.

He turned toward her, his coffee brown eyes almost black with emotion. "It was shortly after that incident that Stacey started dyeing her hair, adopting her outrageous fashion style. Obviously to protest her father's treatment in the only way she knew how, by embarrassing the other Rivals. It didn't endear her to anyone. In fact, both Granddad and Dad thought less of Wayne for being unable to control his daughter."

"Poor Wayne."

"Yes, poor Wayne. I loved my dad. He was always so good to me. So was Granddad." But Craig was ashamed of them both for their treatment of Wayne, ashamed of himself for not righting the wrong before he'd left for Europe. "He probably saw his life slipping away, nothing to show for all his years of loyal service to a family that neither loved nor appreciated him. He was going to hurt me in the only way he could—by stealing the Purity."

"Apparently," Lyssa reminded him, "he changed his mind at the last minute. You knew him, Craig. So did I. No matter what, I don't think he would have gone through with the theft."

He wanted to believe she was right, wanted to believe a part of Wayne's desperation was his own fault for thoughtlessly delaying the partnership. He stood, pulling her to her feet. "Come on. It's getting late."

Rain was falling in torrents as they left the hospital. Wind whipped water across the ground with the force of a high-pressured hose, sweeping leaves and debris away in wide cleansing swaths. Lyssa felt a similar cleansing had taken place inside her, a decontaminating of her soul, a sense of her original self emerging from the grit and grime of the past few years. Kevin no longer had any power over her; the only emotion he stirred in her was abhorrence.

But as they drove through the wet Seattle streets toward her hotel, she felt suddenly drained, at the limit of her endurance for this day. She said good-night at her door, accepted Craig's almost brotherly kiss without inviting him inside. He seemed to understand her reticence. She wasn't sure she did. Wasn't sure why she was pushing him away.

Monday

CRAIG CALLED JACKSON around nine that morning. He told the detective about Kevin's confession and about his own efforts to get Wayne's body exhumed.

"Under the circumstances, I think that can be arranged," Jackson said. There was a pause, then he added, "I was going to phone you in a while. Kevin

Carlyle didn't make it through the night. A blood clot, as I understand it.''

"Have you told Lyssa?"

"Not yet."

"Let me?"

"If that's what you want."

It wasn't what he wanted, but he figured it was probably better that she hear it from someone who cared about her than on the news.

Half an hour later, Lyssa let him into her hotel room. Her packed suitcase stood ready by the door. Was she walking out of his life forever? The thought went through his heart like a jagged knife. Then it occurred to him that he had one way of hanging on to her, at least for long enough to figure out whether they had any future. "Looks like you're ready to go."

"Yes. I don't want to miss another flight."

"You've got a couple hours yet, and I have a proposition for you."

Lyssa's look was wary, and he guessed she was afraid he was going to ask her for something she couldn't give. Herself. It saddened him. "What kind of proposition?" she asked.

"Strictly business. Would you be interested in leasing the Purity? Before you say yea or nay, I've checked the feasibility of it with my insurance agent, and you'd have to pay some hefty premiums. Plus, I'll insist on a written agreement."

This man was always surprising her. Lyssa's wariness dwindled. "What kind of terms in the agreement?"

He grinned, and she felt her heartbeat flutter. "My demands are pretty simple," he said. "The only provision is that in the event I should marry before your grandmother's death, the lease automatically becomes null and void and you must return the Purity before my wedding day."

Lyssa couldn't bear the thought of him being married to someone else. But imagining *herself* in another marriage stole her very breath.

Craig was waiting. "Well?"

"I accept. How soon before it's arranged?"

"Would today be soon enough?"

"You can't do the paperwork that fast."

"No, but I can fax the initial papers tomorrow and send you a copy of the originals as soon as they're filed."

"I accept."

Craig hated ruining her happy mood, but he could no longer put off telling her about Kevin.

The news of Kevin's death left Lyssa more conscious than ever of life's fragility. "Before we go, I want to call my mother."

Lyssa told her mother all that had occurred—with the exception of her night with Craig—and explained that she was fine and planned to return later in the day.

"I'm delighted to hear that Grandy is better."

"She's driving me crazy, asking to see you—and the Purity." A touch of reproof sharpened Roxanne's tone. "And . . . Craig."

Guilt nagged Lyssa, and she sighed. "Mother, Craig's offered to lease me the Purity. I'm picking it up in a few minutes and bringing it with me this afternoon. I'm going to tell Grandy the truth."

But which truth? she wondered as she replaced the receiver. That she cared for Craig? Probably loved him, but could never marry him? Would never marry anyone again? Even if she was so inclined, her family would never accept Craig Rival, and she wouldn't subject him to her family's scorn. How could she enter into a marriage with those kinds of odds stacked against it?

She spun around to face him.

"How's your family?" He grabbed hold of her luggage.

"Doing fairly well." She gave him an abbreviated rundown.

"Good." Craig held the door as she preceded him. "I'm afraid mine will sever our nebulous family ties altogether when she hears that the police are going ahead with the exhumation and that Kevin implicated Wayne in his plan to steal the Purity."

"Will she be at the office when we get there?"

"Probably."

LYSSA DISCOVERED THAT Rival Gems International was much like other elegant establishments she'd encountered over the years in her line of work. She and Craig found Stacey and Ginger in the showroom, putting an order together.

Stacey lifted her flat-black hair away from her face, raked Lyssa with a chilly glance and asked in a contemptuous voice, "What's *she* doing here?"

Ginger's eyes widened, darting from her cousin to her boss who was scowling at Stacey. "I'll get some coffee."

"Not for me," Craig called after her. Then he said coldly to Stacey, "I'd like a word with you. In private."

Her hands landed on her hips, jangling the profusion of bracelets on her wrists. "If this is about the same business as last night, my answer is still no."

"In private."

With an exasperated grunt, she followed him into his office.

Ginger returned from the back room with two steaming mugs.

Lyssa thanked her, then strode to the windows at the far end of the room and glanced at the smattering of clouds dotting the otherwise blue sky. Yesterday's storm had given the city a freshly scrubbed appearance, reminding her of the cleansing sensation she'd experienced last night.

Wasn't there another layer of old grit right here that needed whisking away? She wheeled around and walked along the counter to where her cousin was checking pieces of jewelry against an order form. Ginger glanced up questioningly. There were soft blue smudges beneath her eyes and she immediately started nibbling at her fingernail. Had she heard about Kevin and spent the night in tears?

"Did you know that Kevin died during the night?" Lyssa's question evoked a shocked look from Ginger. Deciding not to hold anything back, Lyssa told her everything that Kevin had been up to. The color had drained completely from Ginger's face by the time Lyssa finished.

Ginger brought her hand to her mouth. "Oh, my. This beats all."

Didn't it just? Lyssa started to turn away, but Ginger said, "Lyssa."

"What?"

"Thanks for telling me. I know it wasn't easy for you." Ginger fingered her large hoop earring. "And I'm glad Kevin didn't . . . you know."

"Are you?"

"Yes. I'll never forgive myself for letting a man come between us. But I thought I loved him. Gullible me, I believed anything and everything he told me. To think I felt sorry for him." She sighed. "He blamed you and Uncle Denny when Savage Cologne ousted him as their spokesperson. Savage is a very family-oriented business. Kevin hadn't signed his contract before he and I— I'm sure his morals lost him the job, but at the time, I thought it was just your way of getting back at me."

"You should have known better."

"Yes, I should have known better about a lot of things, like Kevin marrying me as soon as your divorce was final. I should have known better than to follow him to Seattle. Should have known better than to give him my life savings.

"It wasn't long before we were dead broke." Ginger's mouth curved in a self-deprecating smirk. "We both thought my getting the job here was sweet irony. We used to laugh about it. Me, being able to hold the Purity anytime I wanted, when the DeHavilands couldn't. I quit laughing when Kevin dumped me for…someone else. Especially when Uncle Denny showered me with love and support. That made me look at what I'd done to you. I really regret it, Lyssa."

She seemed sincere. Maybe her father was right. Maybe it was time she forgave Ginger—so they could both heal from the wound Kevin had inflicted. Trusting her was another matter. *That* Ginger would have to earn.

But wasn't this a beginning? Deciding to take it as the first giant step on the road to forgiveness, Lyssa gave her cousin a nod and a smile.

Ginger smiled, too, and the wariness in her eyes melted.

Lyssa felt a new lightness in her heart mingle with the last of her reservations. All the hurt hadn't gone, but it was dissipating. She wandered over to a large antique showcase. "Is this the famous Collection?"

"Yes. The Purity is near the windows."

Lyssa quickly scanned the impressive pieces displayed in the case until her gaze came to rest on the necklace that her grandmother attributed with the power to ensure happy marriages. It *was* impressive. She bent at the waist, taking a long hard look at the Purity. The diamonds seemed less blue than normal in the dull daylight. And the gold at the edge of the clasp had a tiny flaw like the— The heat drained from Lyssa's face. Oh, no. It couldn't be. But it was—she'd swear it was.

The faux!

Chapter Fourteen

Lyssa clutched the counter as if she were standing on two broken legs. Warmth had drained from her face and her body, and she knew her mouth was hanging open.

"What's the matter?" Ginger asked, but her attention swung to Craig's office as the door banged open.

"The man confessed. Isn't that enough for you? Why must you disturb Dad?" Stacey stormed into the showroom, bracelets jangling like warning bells. Twin splotches of red showed through her ghostly pale makeup, and tears streaked her face.

A moment later Craig appeared. "It's not up to me. It's up to the police."

Shaking her head, she grasped a black coat from the brass coat tree and, with it billowing about her like a vampire's cape, fled into the foyer.

"Craig?" The word seemed wrenched from Lyssa's throat in a hoarse whisper.

He frowned, staring at the door as if Stacey would reappear at any second.

"Craig." This time Lyssa's voice held urgency, weight.

His frown deepened as he turned toward her.

She had Ginger's attention again, too. "What's wrong?"

The air in the showroom had a sudden thick expectancy, a foreboding gloom. Lyssa thought she might be ill. "The Purity. I think it's my copy."

"No way." Craig looked incredulous. Then relieved. "I placed the Purity in that case myself three days ago."

"Are you sure it was the real one?"

"Positive. I double-checked."

Her certainty faltered. She glanced into the case again. There was no mistaking the flawed clasp, nor the lack of blue in the stones. With sickening sureness, she glanced at him again. "When was the last time you looked at it?"

He considered. When had C.J. and Teri been here? Of course. The same day he'd placed it in the case, the day of the hit-and-run. "Friday."

"Please, look at it now."

Distress darted through Ginger's eyes and, gnawing at her fingernail, she scooted out of Craig's path as he hastened to the case and unlocked the back panel. With his heart beating erratically, he retrieved the necklace, straightened and laid it on the counter. The weight had felt right, but to his naked eye the stones seemed less blue. His mouth went dry. He pulled his loupe from his pocket.

A second later, he realized he was staring at zircons. The bottom dropped out of his stomach. Swearing, he nearly ran Ginger down as he dashed to the vault. No Purity. In a panic, he rechecked the case. Examined the lock. No signs of tampering. How could this be? Wayne was dead. Kevin was dead. Who had the Purity?

"Ginger." Craig's face was red, his voice icy. "What do you know about this?"

"Me?" Ginger cringed like a cornered mouse, and tears sprang to her eyes. "I knew it. Ever since I found it that day, I knew it was a bad omen. And now I'll be blamed—"

Lyssa frowned at her. "What do you mean, *since you found it that day? What day?*"

Ginger snuffled, peering through damp lashes, swallowing as if her throat were clogged. Her creamy complexion was splotched from emotion. "The—the morning after Wayne died. I f-found the Purity in the e-empty Collection case. Just lying in a heap. Like somebody had tossed it there."

"Wasn't the case locked?" A nerve in Craig's jaw twitched.

"No. It was empty."

Craig fought to curb his impatience. "What time of day did you find the Purity?"

"Around 11:00 a.m." Ginger's voice was strident.

"Was Kevin Carlyle here that morning?"

"H-how did you know?"

Craig didn't answer, but said to Lyssa, "That explains how the Purity was returned, and how it got back into the vault."

Lyssa glanced at Ginger, recalling she'd lied about the necklace never being out of the vault. Had she lied to protect Wayne—or Kevin? Lyssa felt a prickling at her neck. With Kevin's unmasking, she'd thought the clowns were all accounted for, but it seemed there was another player in the game. Her pulse skipped. Was it Ginger?

Or someone else?

Ginger was afraid of something. Was it that she'd be accused of the theft, or that she'd be caught with the Purity? Lyssa needed to know. "Did you take the Purity, Ginger?"

Ginger flinched as if she'd been slapped. She fled into the back room and was back in a flash, a large handbag in tow. Emptying its contents on the counter, she glared at Lyssa. "I swear I don't know who took it or where it is. Would you like to search me?"

Craig dragged his taut fingers through his hair. "Who's been here this morning?"

"Lots of people." Ginger seemed to be grasping at her dignity. She lifted her chin and sniffed. "Let's see . . . Dav—Mr. Lundeen—was here to see Stacey. And Ms. Temple to see you. There were a few one-time buyers. Oh, and Teri came in, too, but not with her boss. No, they weren't here together."

"Did you leave anyone unattended today?"

Ginger said quickly, "Only Ms. Temple and only for a minute or so, while I answered the telephone."

Lyssa gathered her coat and her purse. "I say we pay a quick visit to Ms. C.J. Temple."

Craig nodded. With her mysterious buyer for the Purity and her unscrupulous business tactics, C.J. was the obvious starting point. "Ginger, call the police," he instructed. Report the theft and answer their questions as best you can. We should be back before they've gone."

"Should I tell them where you are?" Ginger lifted the telephone receiver.

"Not unless they ask specifically," Craig said. "They might think we're interfering with their case."

Ginger's expression seemed to say, "Aren't you?"

"What we're trying to do—" Lyssa tugged on her coat "—is recover the necklace before it's dismantled and sold."

"If it isn't already too late," added Craig.

"Don't say that," Lyssa reprimanded him as they exited the offices and hurried into the hallway. "What do you think?"

Craig wasn't certain what he thought. He was back to suspecting them all—his clerk and his cousin and his lawyer and his main competitor and her assistant—of aiding and abetting the murder of his uncle and the near murder of Lyssa. And of stealing the Purity.

TEMPLE'S TREASURES & Trinkets, Inc., was located on the second floor of the Columbia SeaFirst Center Building. The shop reflected C.J.'s taste: austere decor so subtle as to be almost nonexistent. The display cases held two of Lyssa's original designs and one of her faux pieces. Which, she pondered, did C.J. consider the treasure and which the trinket?

They asked to speak to C.J., but it was Teri who appeared from the back room a moment later. She would never acquire the sense of style and taste that were inbred in her boss, and the gracious room seemed to emphasize this.

The shop cried champagne and caviar. Even in a designer suit, Teri looked like beer and pretzels. Lyssa preferred her that way. Down to earth. Genuine. Honest and caring. Dark smudges beneath her eyes attested to a poor night's sleep, and her eager greeting and immediate concern for Lyssa's health made her realize she'd probably caused her friend undue worry.

"Hi. What's going on?" Teri had heard about Kevin, but seemed at as much a loss for words on the subject as Lyssa.

Craig asked for C.J.

"She's not here."

"Where is she? It's urgent that we speak with her."

His gruff tone had Teri's eyebrows lifting. "Well, she had several appointments." She checked the time. "She ought to be at Ben Marlowe's now."

"Ben Marlowe, the gem cutter?" Craig's lips thinned into twin white lines.

Teri nodded. "Would you like me to call?"

"No! Not unless I miss her."

Back in the car, Lyssa asked, "Do you think we'll find the necklace intact?" There was a tremor in her voice.

Craig glanced at her, knowing she was no more interested in the actual worth of the necklace from a monetary view than he, and she was probably feeling the same emptiness he was of discovering someone had stolen a piece of his family history, an irreplaceable part of his heritage. No insurance premium could cover that. He pressed his foot harder on the gas pedal and careered around a bus. "Let's hope C.J. took it and we'll get to her in time."

"But what if she didn't take it?" Lyssa fidgeted beside him.

He hated the alternatives and suspected she did, too. "I guess we'll have to let the police handle it." His mouth was dry, his palms damp, his nerves frayed as he pulled into a parking garage. Moments later, they were inside Ben Marlowe's gem shop.

They were told he was with a customer and asked to wait. Craig waited half a second, then pushed past the receptionist and charged into the man's office. Ben and his customer, a diamond-draped dowager, were startled by the intrusion. The woman drew back as if she expected Craig to demand she hand over her jewelry.

Ben, a ruddy-complected man whose black hair and bushy eyebrows were thick with gray, clearly recognized Craig and just as clearly was affronted by his rudeness. He braced his stocky body. "What's the meaning of this, Mr. Rival?"

Craig winced, immediately contrite. "Excuse me, Mr. Marlowe—Ben. I had reason to believe you were with C.J. Temple and—"

"Ms. Temple?" Ben interrupted, his sharp brown eyes impatient. "Sure, she was here. You missed her by an hour or so."

Lyssa felt her heart drop to the level of her toes. Was it too late?

"What did she bring you?" Worry laced Craig's words. His face was red, his jaw taut.

Ben lifted his stocky body back and away from Craig, his bushy eyebrows shooting up. "Really, Mr. Rival, I can assure you I am not in the habit of divulging my customers' business."

All fear and indignation left the dowager's face. She leaned forward, her keen eyes eager with curiosity.

Feeling the situation going from bad to worse, Lyssa called up what she hoped was her most engaging smile, and said, "I apologize for this intrusion, Mr. Marlowe. Please forgive us. But it's vital that we know if Ms. Temple has brought you some half-carat diamonds and one two-carat diamond for cutting. They'd be flawless stones."

Two seconds passed. His eyebrows twitched, then lowered. Lyssa said a silent prayer.

Ben's expression grew less defensive. Finally he replied, "I suppose you realize you're putting me in an embarrassing position here. Ms. Temple and you are both my valued customers."

Craig nodded, but a nerve jumped in his cheek. He spoke with controlled calm, and Lyssa knew he was selecting his words with care, even if they weren't exactly honest. "It's just that these could be stones we're both interested in."

The dowager's ears seemed to perk up at this information, giving her the look of a bejeweled poodle.

Ben considered another moment. "This is highly irregular, but I suppose I can say that she didn't bring me anything."

Relief flooded through Lyssa and she could see it on Craig's face, as well.

The dowager frowned, and her ring-laden hands landed on her hips. "Really, Ben! Isn't that C.J. person the one who's bringing in the diamonds today that you promised me?"

A tinge of red spiraled up Ben Marlowe's neck. "No, Mrs. Smythe."

The fire was back in Craig's face, and Lyssa's stomach pinched. Was Ben lying? Or just angry at the position they'd put him in, at their unprofessionalism, their veiled innuendos about C.J. Temple? She couldn't tell. But there wasn't another thing they could do about it. They'd already trodden the boundaries of libel.

They rode back to the office in silence. Expecting the police might still be there, they were surprised to find the office locked. Ginger was gone.

As they entered the showroom, the phone was ringing. It was Detective Jackson. Craig told him about the theft and asked if it had been reported.

Jackson wasn't at the office, but promised he'd check and get back to them on it. "You think Carlyle switched the necklaces before he kicked off?"

If that was so, the Purity might be lost to them forever. There wasn't one scenario that made him any more comfortable. His head felt ready to burst from inactivity. "I couldn't tell you, Detective."

"Maybe there's another snake in the grass."

"Maybe."

"Interesting. Anyway, I wanted to touch base with you on the autopsy. It's being done later today. I pulled your uncle's medical records, and I see he was taking digitalis."

"Yes, I knew that." The implication slammed into Craig's skull. "Are you saying you think the coroner will find an overdose?"

"I think it's a safe bet."

Craig felt chilled. Did Stacey already know this? Was that why she'd been so upset about the autopsy? Was that why she'd stormed out of here? His head throbbed with questions. Was Stacey the distraught daughter, or Kevin Carlyle's partner? Had she made a quick getaway this morning with the necklace stuffed in her pocket? More than anything, he needed to find out. He gave Jackson his car-phone number and asked to be notified about the theft report, then hung up.

"Did Ginger report the theft?"

He shrugged. "Jackson will find out. Meantime, I've got to see Stacey."

Lyssa rolled her eyes. "That's one encounter I'd rather avoid. Why don't you drop me back at the condo and see her on your own?"

He did as she asked, promising to return in an hour, but he'd been gone less than five minutes when the doorbell to the condo rang. Lyssa hurried to the door. "Forget your—?"

Ginger stood on the stoop, looking like something the cat had dragged in, then changed its mind about. She shouldered past Lyssa and into the house. "Oh, Lyssa, I know Craig thinks I stole the Purity, and when the police find out I was involved with Kevin, they'll think I sicced him on Wayne. But it wasn't like that. You have to believe me."

The door was wide open, the cold wind spitting wet raindrops against her back. Ginger hadn't asked to see Craig. It meant she knew he wasn't there. Fear crept around Lyssa's heart. "Did you report the Purity's theft?"

Ginger's brown eyes were awash with tears. "N-no. I'm scared the police—"

Lyssa took a step backward. Despite their tentative truce, by not reporting the theft, Ginger had only reinforced Lyssa's distrust of her. Why was she really here?

"Lyssa," Ginger said in a pleading voice. "We're flesh and blood. You have to help me."

Lyssa took another step back. Wind railed against her, blowing her hair around her face. "Ginger, I can't protect you from the law if you're guilty of murder."

The threatening tears rolled freely down Ginger's cheeks. "I couldn't hurt a hair on Wayne Rival's head," she said, sobbing. "I loved him." She swiped at her damp face with the back of her hand and fixed

Lyssa with a soggy gaze. "But I think I can guess who might have."

RUSH HOUR WAS WELL underway by the time Craig exited the West Seattle freeway onto Harbor Avenue. Menacing clouds weighed heavy in the sky, looking like grimy petticoats about to sweep over the city. Wind, blowing in from Puget Sound, pummeled the Lexus. He tapped his brake, slowed, then merged with the thick traffic.

The only thing he felt good about at the moment was that Lyssa was safe in his condo. He gripped the steering wheel, his thoughts as dark as the sky. He'd just gotten off the car phone with Jackson who'd told him Ginger hadn't reported the theft, and that he'd dispatched a patrol car to her house which was just up the hill from Stacey's.

David also lived in this section of town. Craig blew out a disgusted breath and cursed himself for being a fool. He'd trusted his cousin and his old friend, believed they were having a love affair, when in reality Stacey must have been involved with Kevin Carlyle. A foul taste filled his mouth. He wasn't just a fool, he was ten times a fool, and his denial had cost him the Purity.

He drove past ships in dry dock, past the open bay stretching to Seattle, and around the bend onto Alki Avenue. Beach houses and apartment buildings crowded together, hugging the hillside to his left; sandy beach stretched along his right. The fierce breeze was whipping the waters of Puget Sound into a frenzy of whitecaps, swirling leaves and an odd paper cup into his path.

But if Stacey was involved with Carlyle, where did that leave David? He was involved. Had to be. He'd lied about drawing up the document between Lyssa and Wayne. The bad taste slid into Craig's stomach and curdled. Was what he'd seen between Stacey and David genuine? Had they used Kevin to get rid of Lyssa and Wayne? Used him so that they could steal the Purity?

The car in front of him ground to a stop, turn signal flashing. Craig braked, his patience thinning with every delay. He'd give anything in the world to be wrong. But he knew he wasn't. The aroma of fresh fried lingcod drew his attention toward Spud's Fish and Chips, a favorite eating spot since his childhood. What a long time ago that suddenly seemed.

He swung his gaze forward. Out of the corner of his eye, he saw a woman—her cape and smooth auburn hair flowing in the wind—leaving the restaurant. He glanced at her. A band of lightning arced from overhead, followed by a thunderous clap. He jumped as if the flashing bolt had struck him.

C.J.!

She hurried across the road ahead. Frantic to cut her off, all Craig could do was sit there, craning his neck to see around the car in front of him. "Damn!"

He hit his horn. Finally, the car blocking his passage turned. Craig jammed his foot to the floor. The Lexus lurched ahead, tires squealing. There was no sign of C.J. She'd gotten away. But unless he was sorely mistaken, he knew where she was going—Stacey's house.

"CAN'T YOU GO any faster?" Lyssa asked anxiously.

"Not in this traffic, lady," the cab driver answered. "Not with this power outage. It's slowed us to a crawl."

Wringing her hands, she swallowed a frustrated scream and glanced at the industrial buildings below the freeway, wishing she was certain her cousin had told her the truth. Wondering why Ginger had immediately rushed off into the night without so much as a goodbye. Where had she gone?

Afterward, as she'd sat alone in Craig's condo, contemplating what Ginger's revelation might mean about the Purity, Lyssa had been swept with an awful foreboding. An inexplicable sense that something was wrong.

She tried to reach him on his car phone, then at Stacey's house. But no one had answered. Maybe Stacey wasn't home. But then, where was Craig? On his way back to the condo? Were they, even now, passing on opposite sides of the freeway? Or—she began to shake—maybe Craig had run into serious trouble.

CRAIG ROUNDED THE BEND that changed Alki Avenue into Beach Drive. The road was all but clear of traffic. Still no sign of C.J. She couldn't have disappeared so quickly, unless she'd pulled into one of the few driveways ahead. Most likely Stacey's.

Wind whined across his car, sending a chill down his spine. He slowed the Lexus as Stacey's three-story clapboard house came into view. Only Stacey's car occupied the driveway. Had C.J. parked somewhere else? There was an inexplicable prickling at his neck. He decided not to park in the drive, either. He drove past the house to the next and the next before he pulled to a stop.

He grasped the door handle, then hesitated. Maybe he should call Jackson back and tell him ... Tell him what? That he *suspected* his cousin had stolen the Purity? That he *suspected* she was about to sell it to their main competitor? No. They might get away with it if he waited for the police to arrive.

Hastening from the car, he was assaulted by the biting, forceful breeze hurling in from the Sound. He hunched his shoulders and, feeling like a spy in a grade-B film, hurried toward Stacey's house. Darkness was closing in, but neither streetlights nor house lights came on. Was the power out?

He ran across Stacey's tiny front lawn, stepped into her flower garden and stopped, leaning against the edge of the house. He swallowed hard, counted to ten, then peered around the corner. His heart skipped two beats. Stacey's car was still alone in the driveway.

Thunder rumbled overhead and dollops of rain beat against Craig's face, stealing inside his coat collar. He hunched his shoulders and ran for the porch.

Lightning blinked behind him, followed immediately by a crack of thunder. He lifted his hand to knock on the door. From inside the house came the sound of a loud bang.

Craig jolted. Was that a gunshot?

Swearing, he grabbed the knob. It was unlocked. He shoved the door inward. "Stacey!"

The interior hall was dark, shadowed. He reached for the light switch. The only response was an echoing click. The darkness remained absolute. With his pulse racing, he stepped forward, groping the wall.

Lightning flashed, illuminating the hall and his surroundings with an eerie clarity. He spotted Stacey, not three feet ahead. Lying on the floor in a pool of blood.

Chapter Fifteen

The cabdriver pulled to a stop on Beach Drive. The taxi's headlights offered the only illumination on the whole street, as far as Lyssa could see in either direction. Rain and wind whipped against the car, and she was glad she'd changed into jeans and borrowed a fleece-lined denim jacket she'd found in Craig's closet.

She peered out at the dark house across the street from the taxi, then returned her gaze to the cabby. Farther down the road, a car reflected in the taxi's headlights caught her attention. Craig's Lexus. "I think this is the wrong house."

"This is the number you gave me, lady. You want to check it again?" The cabby started to turn into the driveway.

"No. Don't do that," Lyssa cried out, uncertain why the thought of shining headlights across the darkened house alarmed her. But it did. "Please, drive ahead up to that black car."

"Okay." The cabby shrugged and did as directed, stopping behind the Lexus.

She started to hand over her fare, then snatched it back beyond his reach. The Lexus was the right color, but was it Craig's? "I think I know that car, but I can't be certain without looking inside. Do you have a flashlight I could borrow?''

He looked at the money, then her. ''Hey, lady, don't give me no trouble.''

The implied threat rattled her; the man was twice her size. Nonetheless, she lifted her chin defiantly. ''No trouble. I just need that flashlight.''

''The fare covers pickups and deliveries, lady. Anything else costs extra.''

''How much?''

He looked at her again, this time with a sly, assessing sweep of his cool gray eyes. ''Twenty.''

At least he had a flashlight, she thought with satisfaction. Unfortunately, he knew she was desperate. And in a hurry. ''How about ten?''

''Twenty. Take it or leave it.''

''All I have is fifteen.''

''Let's see the money.''

''Let's see the flashlight.''

He reached into the glove box and withdrew a hand-size, black-and-copper-colored plastic flashlight that had probably cost him six bucks, tops. Holding it between his thumb and forefinger, he dangled it just beyond her reach as she'd done with the money, and grinned.

She frowned. ''Does it work?''

''Brand-new.'' He flicked it on and shined it in her face.

She grimaced, blinking in annoyance. The beam wasn't brilliant, but it was better than nothing, and at the moment she'd willingly have paid double for one with half its output. They made the exchange. ''Would you stick around a moment longer?'' she asked. ''If this car belongs to my friend, then you can go. Otherwise, I'll need a ride back into town."

"What are you planning to pay me with, if I already got all you had on you?"

"I have more cash at my house."

He took precious seconds deciding whether or not to believe her, then, with a grin that said he'd drive her to the moon and back if she wanted to pay for it, he nodded. "Okay. Sure. I'll wait."

Grumbling to herself about the lack of human kindness in the world these days, she stepped into the rain, bent into the wind and hustled to the Lexus. Although the interior was gray like Craig's car, she felt no reassurance. What were the odds that Stacey's neighbor would have a car exactly like Craig's? She couldn't even guesstimate and, no matter how slim the chances, she dared not rule out the possibility. If only there was some *thing,* some recognizable something.

She played the light beam along the dashboard again. There. What was that beige coupon nestled against the windshield? Checking closer, she saw it was a parking stub from the garage they'd used earlier while visiting Ben Marlowes. Why wasn't she relieved? Why did the anxious sensation keep grabbing her insides?

Maybe she should ask the cabby to accompany her to Stacey's house. No. She was being ridiculous. It was the darkness. Lyssa dismissed the cab. But as he drove out of sight, leaving her alone on the empty street, wind and rain and trepidation swept over her.

Where were the masses that crowded the freeway such a short distance away? Didn't any of those people live here? Was no one at home? She cast a glance at the Lexus, then at the house beside it. The curtains were drawn. To keep out the night? Or to hold in its secrets? Was Craig inside? She shone the flashlight beam on the brass numbers beside the front door. They didn't match those she'd copied from Craig's address book.

Stacey's house must be the one the cabby had taken her to originally. But if that were so, why had Craig parked here? He'd had no reason to conceal his visit to Stacey's. Had he?

She started toward the house. She could neither explain nor rid herself of the feeling that something was wrong. Why hadn't he returned to the condo? He'd promised to be back within the hour, and yet, more than two hours had passed before she'd started out after him.

Lyssa trembled. Her face was slick with rain, her clothing damp, the wind biting, but her shaking was born of a marrow-rattling chill as old as life and death. Inexplicably, she felt whatever had delayed Craig was dire.

Without an idea of how she'd gotten there, Lyssa found herself staring at the house she suspected was Stacey Rival's. It loomed three stories tall, a narrow, imposing structure from another era that now stood shadowed and gloomy against the hillside. The drapes were not drawn; yet no lights were visible through any of the windows. But this was the house, and Lyssa knew, with some indefinable, flesh-prickling certainty, that she would find Craig inside.

Wind shoved at her back, seeming intent on hurrying her to the porch, as if she were urgently needed. The sensation escalated her apprehension, stole her very breath. At the door, she started to knock, but some inner warning stopped her. She tried the knob.

Locked. But there had to be a way inside. She leapt off the porch and stood back surveying the house.

From inside, a beam of light fanned across the large second-floor window above the portico. Someone was inside.

Her heart leapt with terror. It was all she could do to keep from crying out Craig's name, so sudden and great was her fear for his life. *Please, don't let me be too late. Don't let me lose Craig when I've only just found him.*

She ran toward the backyard, splaying the light beam ahead. Something grabbed her sore ankle. She tripped. The flashlight flew from her grasp and blinked off. Lyssa hit the ground, the wind knocked from her. She lay still for a second, catching her breath. Then she patted the muddy ground nearby, seeking the flashlight. Her fingers touched a sleek surface, curved as a human cheek, cold as a corpse. Bile rose in her throat. Despite her panic, she located the flashlight and flicked the On switch.

Nothing.

She smacked it against her palm. The feeble beam responded. Cringing, she shined it at the corpse. A pumpkin! She was sitting in a pumpkin patch, tripped by a lacy vine. The idiocy of it roused a hysterical laugh. She choked it down, disentangled her ankle and struggled to her feet.

Praying the light wouldn't fail her, she flicked it over the back of the house, seeking a cellar or basement entrance, a back door of any kind. There was only solid wall and windows. Lyssa swore under her breath, then swiped at her wet, muddy face with a wet, muddy hand. Ignoring the fear swirling inside her, she played the weak beam over the windows one at a time.

Her heart jumped. Like a crooked finger beckoning to her, a snatch of sheer pink drape wagged from between an inch of open window and its frame. The sill was too high off the ground for her to pull herself up and through, but she could reach it if...

She looked around for something to stand on and spied a metal garbage can. Moments later, the up-ended can was wobbling beneath her feet. Mud on the soles of her sneakers and her injured ankle made purchase impossible, and in spite of her every effort toward quiet, the tin popped each time she moved.

The noise couldn't be helped. She had to get inside. Now.

She stuffed the flashlight into one of the coat's deep pockets and shoved the window up—wincing at the accompanying scrape—until there was enough space to fit her body through. Wind howled over the house like a wounded coyote, and Lyssa hoped it covered the racket she was making. She levered herself up the wall and plopped onto the sill with a grunt.

No one came to stop her. Her pulse roaring in her ears, she wriggled across the sill and touched a bed that was shoved close to the wall. She thrust herself at it, misjudged the height and plowed into the edge of the mattress. The impact sent the bed scooting. Lyssa's foot came down hard on the oak floor. Pain zinged through her tender ankle, and she dropped to her bottom, wedged between wall and bed. Something dug into her thigh.

She'd made enough noise to raise the dead. Lyssa's heart thundered. She held her breath. Five seconds passed. Ten. Twenty. No one came. Maybe she was wrong. Maybe the house was empty. Maybe there was some other explanation for Craig's car sitting out on the street.

But what about the light she'd seen in the second-story window? If everything was all right, then why was there such an odd prickling at her nape, an uneasiness in her very bones? Wishing the police hadn't confiscated Craig's gun, Lyssa pushed herself to her knees, gathered the flashlight and spread the beam around the room.

It looked like a tornado had struck. Either Stacey was the world's worst housekeeper or someone had done a frantic search of this room. Recognizing Stacey's black raincoat crumpled on the bed, the pockets turned out, Lyssa knew it was the latter. But what were they searching for?

She levered her hands against the mattress and stood. Her foot landed on something solid. Probably whatever had been jabbing her leg. She directed the flashlight beam at the floor, but couldn't see anything with the blankets and sheets tossed about.

Hauling the covers back onto the bed, she tried again. Something winked at her. Her heart thumped. Could it be? She shoved the bed, widening the gap, and leaned over, grabbing the object. Her heart gave a joyous leap. The Purity. It was still intact. Well, that answered the question of what was being sought.

A loud bump overhead shattered her jubilation. Whoever was up there seemed still to be searching. Surely Stacey wouldn't be searching her own house. Could it be Craig?

Lyssa stuffed the necklace into her coat pocket and hurried to the door. Instinct told her not to reveal herself. Not just yet. Stealthily, she moved out into the pitch-dark hall, pressing the flashlight against her leg, her thumb on the Off switch, in case she needed to douse the light.

She strained to distinguish the sounds coming from upstairs. Her heart beat a tattoo against her ears. Voices? Or was it the wind whispering through the old house? Had she heard Craig? Or had she wanted to hear him so badly she'd imagined she had? She extinguished the flashlight and shoved it into a coat pocket. Best to save what little energy remained in the batteries.

Using the spill of light issuing from the second floor as a guide, she stepped gingerly toward the staircase. Her right foot hit a slick spot. Her leg slid forward. She let out a yelp, threw out her hands and ended up half sprawled, half standing, with one palm flat on the floor... pressed against something liquid and sticky.

Her dry hand found the flashlight. Its feeble beam revealed a dark spot on the floor. Lyssa recoiled. It looked like blood. Fresh blood. Fear shot through her. She brought her trembling hand to her nose and sniffed, instantly identifying the sickly sweet scent. It *was* blood. Her stomach lurched.

A resounding crash echoed across the ceiling.

Her gaze jerked up.

Someone swore.

Lyssa froze. That wasn't Craig. She glanced down at her bloodied hand. Was she staring at Craig's blood? Heartsick with fear, Lyssa got to her feet and fought the urge to dash up the stairs headlong into whatever was going on. There was safety in numbers. Maybe some of the neighbors were home now. But what if they weren't? Dare she waste time running from house to house? No. A telephone would be quicker. A direct route to the police.

Haunted with images of Craig bleeding to death, she located the kitchen. Pent-up air rushed through her taut lips as she spotted the telephone on the counter. She snatched up the receiver and poked 91—

"Put it down. Now!"

Recognizing the voice behind her, Lyssa went as wooden as a totem pole. Had she managed to depress the other 1? She didn't know. She set the phone away from her and spun around. "What are you do—?"

The barrel of a gun was pointed at her heart.

CRAIG CAME TO with a hell of a headache. He touched his hand gingerly to his temple, finding the tender spot, now sticky with his blood, where the bullet had grazed him. Then he remembered his cousin and called out, "Stacey?"

A hand reached through the darkness and touched him. "Here."

She was alive. Craig gave a silent prayer of thanks. They were in the attic, propped against the beanbag chair he'd carried Stacey to just before the woman had shot him and left them both for dead.

The cramped space was as cold as a meat locker, wind stealing through the siding and whining across the roof. Craig reached for his cousin and put his arm around her shoulders. She groaned. Was the wound in her side still seeping blood?

Her head plopped against his shoulder, heavy for such a tiny woman. "I'm sorry, Craig."

"About what?" He held his breath, not certain he wanted to hear all that she had to tell.

"I knew about the faux Purity." Her speech was hesitant. "I lied about Lyssa Carlyle."

"Why?" But Craig suspected he knew.

"To protect Dad. When he told me about Lyssa's proposal, I encouraged him to do it. I was sick of him getting the short end of the stick." She paused and drew a raspy breath. "I really related to the De-Havilands wanting something from the Rivals. Something this family would never give them."

Again, Craig knew that he could not go blameless in this mess. Like a masochist seeking further pain, he couldn't stop himself from asking, "How did it get from that to this?"

"Kevin Carlyle. I'd seen him at the office... with Ginger. One day, he came on to me. Was flattered. He'd just done the cover of *GQ*. I was curious about Lyssa...his name...the same. Small world. I told him about the copy. About Dad's worry that the whole thing was unethical." Craig felt her head turn and he could picture her sad eyes, so like her father's, gazing up at him. She said, "Didn't know Kevin had talked Dad into stealing the Purity. Can't believe Dad... would even consider that."

"That's why Carlyle killed him, Stacey. Wayne couldn't go through with it." She nodded. Craig asked, "How was David involved?"

"Wasn't."

"But someone from Lundeen's office drew up an agreement between Wayne and Lyssa."

She shook her head. "Ploy to placate Dad. Kevin convinced him he could protect himself with a contract. I...I confiscated blank contract from David's office. Kevin forged...signatures." Her voice was alarmingly weak.

Craig regretted having to make her talk. "Shush, you can tell me later, Stacey. Save your energy. Okay?"

"No. Now." She drew a halting breath. "Soon found out Kevin was a pig. Just using me. Must have copied my office keys. I swear I never knew about him and *her*." She sobbed. "I never knew they'd kill Dad. He'd be alive if not for me."

Craig felt the blame as deeply as Stacey. He hugged her gently, fiercely. Would either of them ever come to terms with their parts in Wayne's death? "Why did she shoot you?"

"The Purity. She put it into my coat pocket this morning. I found it when I got home. Hid it..." Stacey's voice trailed off.

The door suddenly swung inward. Craig blinked against the brilliant flash of light that danced across the narrow space and flicked off the exposed rafters, illuminating cobwebs, piled boxes, discarded furnishings and a light bulb that hung from a beam.

The woman came into view, shoving someone else. Another woman. Craig stiffened. Lyssa? His heart dropped to his toes. What was she doing here? Disentangling himself from Stacey, he lurched to his feet and charged for the women.

"Don't try it." She was much shorter than he, and fearless with the revolver in her hand. She pushed it against Lyssa's temple. "Sit back down."

"Damn it, can't you see Stacey needs a doctor?" he railed. "If you've an ounce of compassion, take the Purity and let me call an ambulance."

"Has she regained consciousness, then?"

He thought better of telling her the truth and hoped Stacey was coherent enough not to give herself away. "No."

The woman gave a vile laugh, then thumbed the hammer of the revolver. "Sit down! Now!"

Even in this stingy light, he could see Lyssa's face was white, her eyes like saucers. "Don't shoot her. I'm sitting." He sank back down beside Stacey, his eyes never leaving the gun, all the while aware that Stacey made no sound when he jostled her. He could no longer hear her ragged breathing.

The woman shoved Lyssa at him. She landed sprawled at his feet. He reached for her. "Are you all right?"

"Yes." Lyssa struggled to her knees, so relieved to see him that she nearly forgot about the woman behind them. About the gun. "Are you okay?"

"Shut up!"

Lyssa jerked. She wheeled around and sat next to Craig. She eyed the woman she'd thought was her friend. "Why, Teri?"

Teri, a gleam in her pale blue eyes that was nothing Lyssa had ever seen nor recognized, smiled indulgently. "I wouldn't tell him, but I do believe I'd like you to know. Where should I start? Should I go all the way back to our junior high prom, where you danced all night with Lonny Sanderson, knowing that I was mad for him? Did you know that I cried my heart out for a week afterward? Did you care? No. Because you kept on stealing my men all through high school and college. But when I met Kevin Carlyle, I swore he was one man you wouldn't have."

"Kevin?" Lyssa frowned, trying to take this in.

"Yes, I met him first. But I underestimated his greed. He saw a snapshot of us and asked about you. Like an idiot, I told him all about the DeHavilands. Next thing I knew, he was dating you behind my back."

Lyssa hadn't thought anything else could shock her. She'd been wrong. "Why didn't you tell me? I wouldn't have dated him, much less married him."

"Kevin talked me into keeping quiet. That man could talk a bear out of honey. Before you start feeling too sorry for me, though, I should tell you I had the satisfaction of sleeping with your husband nearly every day after you returned from your honeymoon."

If Teri had meant to hurt her with this revelation, she'd failed. All Lyssa felt was disgust. "What about Mason? I thought—"

"*I* thought the old goat had money. I knew that was the only way of winning Kevin once and for all. But Mason had the last laugh. Unbeknownst to me, he had mortgaged everything he owned. The state and the bank took it all. I killed him for nothing. I was back at square one. You had Kevin, I had zip."

A chill wrapped around Lyssa heart. If Teri had killed Mason, what would stop her from killing the three of them?

"C.J.'s right about sentiment," Teri ranted on. "It won't buy you diddly. When you finally dumped Kevin, I talked him into coming to Seattle. The jerk brought Ginger with him, so I was still sharing him. Ginger had enough money to keep him happy for a while. When that ran out, he dumped her for Stacey. But the last straw was when I caught him coming on to C.J.

"I was sick of sharing him. That's when it came to me. Why not use his influence with Stacey to rip off the Collection? Your desire to copy the Purity gave us an even better idea. With an available copy, and Craig in Europe, it seemed foolproof. We'd just exchange necklaces, sell the real Purity to C.J.—who wants it so badly she'll take it any way she can get it—then when the time was right, help ourselves to the rest, plant some lesser piece in Ginger's apartment, and goodbye good old U.S. of A.''

"What went wrong?" Craig asked.

"You screwed it up." Teri sneered. "Giving Wayne a full partnership for his birthday. He panicked. Figured you'd withdraw the partnership offer if you discovered the Purity had been copied on his authority. He was going to destroy the copy. Kevin employed a little damage control."

Lyssa sighed. "So Kevin killed Wayne and then came after me because I'd spotted him in his car outside Windance."

"I told him to forget it, but he was obsessed with silencing you. And now you've stolen him from me, too." She closed the gap between them. "Turnabout is fair play. Tell your lover boy goodbye, Lyssa."

"You can't hope to get away with this." Craig tried tugging Lyssa behind him, but she resisted, wresting his hands from her arms. What was the matter with her? "C.J. will know it was you, Teri."

Teri shrugged. "So what? Before any of you are even missed, I'll have sold the Purity, and be enjoying the beaches of Rio, with a new name, a whole new identity."

Lyssa plunged her hand into her pocket, wrapping her fingers around the necklace, edging away from Craig. "How are you planning to do that? Stacey's unconscious. Maybe dead. And you don't know where she put the Purity."

"I've got all night to hunt for it." Teri aimed the revolver at Craig's head and pulled back the hammer.

Craig stiffened. Ice flowed through Lyssa's veins.

Teri smiled at her. "But first I'm going to enjoy watching you watch Mr. Stuffed Shirt die."

"If you want the Purity," Lyssa shouted, yanking the necklace from her pocket and heaving it at Teri, "here, catch!"

Teri swung the gun at Lyssa. Craig kicked at her hand. The gun discharged. The bullet went wild. The Purity struck Teri across the bridge of her nose. She cried out in pain. The gun fired again.

This bullet zinged past Craig's ear. Before Teri could get off another shot, he tackled her. Teri shrieked. The revolver flew from her grasp and clattered into the corner. Lyssa dived for it.

Teri was quickly subdued. For the second time in two weeks, Lyssa used her rusty macramé skills, tying both Teri's hands behind her back. Lyssa threw herself into Craig's waiting arms. "I'm okay," he reassured her. "I'm not hurt. The bullets missed me."

"There's blood on your cheek." Lyssa touched it gingerly, wincing as if she could feel the pain as much as he. A banging noise from below startled her. She stepped away from Craig. "Someone's at the door. Let's hope it's the police." As she moved, she spotted Stacey slumped in the chair. Lyssa whipped off her coat and thrust it at him. "Better put this around her. I'll have them call for an ambulance." She hurried out.

He could hear the banging now. And light was spilling in as Lyssa hastened down the stairs. Craig grabbed the string attached to the overhead light and pulled. A bright glare momentarily blinded him, but it was a welcome relief from the darkness.

As he turned toward Stacey, he spied something shiny behind a cardboard box. The Purity. In all the excitement, neither of them had even thought of it. Lyssa's concern had been only for him. And for Stacey. Despite his deep concern about his cousin, his heart felt lighter than it had in weeks.

But what was he really elated about? He had the Purity back, but he still didn't have Lyssa. His joy drained as if someone had pulled a plug. Even if he could convince her to give a permanent relationship with him a chance, her family would blast the idea apart. He'd already suffered their rebuffs. He might never overcome their prejudices of his family. What if they never took him to hearth and heart as he wanted them to do? Could he live with that? Could he ask Lyssa to choose between her family and him?

Chapter Sixteen

Tuesday

What was she going to do? Lyssa wondered as she packed her carry-on bag. How was it possible to fall so completely in love with someone in thirteen days? If she weren't so sad, she would have laughed. Possible or not, she had fallen head over heels for Craig Rival and, after almost losing him last night, she knew for certain that despite her family and all her fears about marriage, she was irrevocably committed to him. But love didn't seem to be enough.

They had argued all night about it. He wanted her family to take him into their hearts and love him as a son. He wanted her mother and father to be his mother and father, her uncles to be his uncles. His words rang in her head like a litany: *I won't accept anything else.*

She'd tried reasoning with him, but a part of her still feared the power of outside influences tearing apart whatever life they might build together, and evidently Craig feared that, too. He'd sworn he'd walk away from her before he'd allow her to walk away from her family.

And that's what he'd done. Stormed out, leaving her alone to pack. Alone to travel to the airport.

Why couldn't he understand? Compromise? The DeHavilands had harbored ill feelings for the Rivals since before Lyssa was born. At best, Craig could win their grudging respect. Why couldn't that be enough for him? And yet, if the situation was reversed, would that be enough for her?

She groaned and closed her eyes against the need for Craig. Memories flooded her mind. She recalled their one night of lovemaking, the glorious feel of his hands caressing her naked body, the sweet sound of her name on his lips, the triumphant joining of their bodies that lingered in her mind, teasing her with tendrils of desire, even now. And probably always would.

Outside a car honked. The taxi. Lyssa gathered her luggage. Her heart felt as heavy as the carry-on bag, packed with a sadness that would never lighten. She took one last look around his condo, searing it into her memory, then rushed out to the cab. Tears stung her eyes. She gave the driver the address for Rival Gems International. She'd decided not to take the Purity until the insurance policy and the agreement were signed and filed. Had Craig returned to Harborview to sit by Stacey's bedside, or would he be at the office when she stopped for the faux Purity?

Despite her fear that she would break down if she saw him again, a part of her hoped for the encounter. But he wasn't there. Ginger was at the showroom counter with C.J.

"Nasty business," C.J. said. "I'm still reeling from the shock. You don't look much better than I feel, sweetie."

"I suppose your customer isn't pleased about not getting the Purity." Lyssa's voice was as flat as her spirits.

"Ha! Life is so weird. You aren't going to believe this. I was just telling Ginger all about it. My customer... one of those billionaire Texans. Oil, I suppose.... Anyway, while his wife and he were staying at a ritzy hotel in Miami this weekend, they were robbed at gunpoint. Every speck of jewelry stolen— which is why I never wear the stuff. Scared them both spitless.

"Fortunately, their really pricey pieces were home in the vault, and they've decided that's where they're going to stay." She handed Lyssa a slip of paper with a name and telephone number neatly written on it. "He wants all their genuine pieces copied. I've given them your name and number. Should net us both a pretty penny."

"Thanks, C.J." What an odd turn of events. Lyssa stuffed the slip of paper into her purse. At least she'd have plenty of work to occupy the lonely, empty hours that were to be her future.

Ginger placed a jewelry box on the counter. "I have the faux Purity ready to go, Lyssa."

"Faux...?" C.J.'s attention shifted between the two women, and Lyssa could almost see the wheels turning in her sharp brain. C.J. leaned an arm on the counter. "You made a copy of the Purity? Mind if I take a look?"

"Go ahead." Lyssa nodded at Ginger. "Show her."

A whistle of approval came from C.J. "Say, you wouldn't consider parting with this, would you?"

Would she? No. The faux, by its very existence, denigrated all that the Purity stood for. There was only one right thing to do with the copy. Dismantle it. "I'm sorry, C.J. It's not for sale."

C.J. rolled her eyes. "Don't tell me. More sentimental hooey. Well, if you change your mind, you know where to reach me."

Then Ginger and Lyssa were alone. Lyssa lifted the jewelry case containing the faux Purity. "Well, I have a taxi waiting and a plane to catch."

"Where's Craig? Why isn't he—? I thought—"

Lyssa smiled sadly at her cousin, feeling that they were once again on a comfortable footing and hurrying toward more solid ground. "It's long and complicated."

"I suppose I'm the last one you want giving you advice, but I think you and Craig have something as special as what Wayne and I had. Life is too short, Lyssa. Believe me, I'd give anything to have your chance at love and happiness." Ginger shrugged. "Just think about it."

And Lyssa had done nothing but think about it. All the way to the airport, through ticketing and loading. Filled with melancholy, she settled into her seat. The plane was far from full. The higher prices and time of year, she supposed. In a way, she was relieved not to have anyone seated next to her. She wasn't in the mood for small talk.

She'd better start figuring out how she was going to explain all the lies she'd told her grandmother. The engines roared to life and soon the plane was taxiing down the runway, lifting off. Lyssa closed her eyes, weary from lack of sleep. But instead of Grandy, her mind was filled with thoughts of Craig.

There was no doubting the importance of family to him. She'd seen it in evidence during the long night at

Harborview, watching his worry over Stacey's surgery, his relief afterward, his tenderness toward his cousin when they visited her hospital room. Family love and support and connection was a need they shared, something inbred in them both.

Somehow she had to convince her family to give this man a chance. For her sake. But doubts pressed down on her.

She was jostled as someone sat in the seat beside her, and she turned her face toward the window. She was startled by a muted *clank,* like charms on a bracelet bumping together. The jangle of a chain? She jerked around in the seat. "Craig!"

His easy grin slipped into place, and he leaned close until their foreheads touched. "We have to stop meeting like this."

Not as far as she was concerned. He was the most welcome sight she could imagine. Had he had a change of heart? Or was he here for some other reason? Her mouth was so dry she couldn't swallow. Or speak.

He traced her jawline with his finger. "I've been considering your grandmother's feelings about the Purity and its powers."

Lyssa brushed her cheek against his hand like an affection-hungry cat, telling herself she mustn't. Nothing was settled yet, and if they couldn't come to terms, this could only prolong the hurt of parting.

"It seems a shame to waste a perfectly good enchanted necklace that, according to Grandy, guarantees—no matter what—our long and lasting love." Craig settled back.

"Do you realize that you're certifiable?"

"Crazy? About you—yes."

She smiled, but it held little joy. "Have you finally come to your senses and now agree with me about a compromise?"

"No. I'm not backing down an inch on this issue. I want the whole family or I walk."

The weight in Lyssa's heart seemed to triple. He wasn't seriously planning on confronting her family with her, was he? It made her sad for him. For them. "Don't get your hopes up."

"If you're trying to say no, please just say it."

Tears welled in her beautiful sea green eyes. "I'm not—"

"Good." He kissed her cheek. "Because I took the liberty of calling your family—your mother, your father and your uncles—and asking for your hand in marriage. You see, I figured you weren't taking one important thing into consideration. How can your family not welcome me with open arms when they see that I truly love you, Lyssa? That you truly love me? You do love me, you know."

"I know." But knowing her family, they probably hadn't received him with open arms. In fact, he was probably on this plane thinking he could change their minds if he spoke with them in person. Her stomach was one big knot. But she had to know. "What did my family say when you asked for my hand?"

"They said a lot of things, but eventually, they all agreed on 'Whatever makes Lyssa happy makes us happy.'"

She couldn't believe it. All her life they'd spoken of the Rivals with bitterness and spite. She should have realized their love for her could circumvent anything. And once they got to know Craig—

He interrupted her thoughts. "If you're still worried about Grandy, well, I suspect she'll be the least surprised of all. I look a great deal like my grandfather Channing, and I'd bet the Purity that she saw the resemblance when you introduced me as Craig Smith. I doubt she's ever forgotten the face of the man who took away her wedding necklace."

"I doubt she has, either."

"Hey, you're smiling." He kissed her neck. "*Are* you happy?"

Lyssa laughed. "What do you think?"

Craig swept his leather jacket off his lap, revealing his black briefcase beneath. Had he brought the Purity with him? He unlocked the lid and she saw immediately that she'd guessed wrong. The case contained only one tiny jeweler's box. Craig reached for it.

"The DeHavilands aren't the only ones with a family heirloom. This was made for my great-great-grandmother by my great-great-grandfather. It's been in my family for four generations. Will you wear it as my wife?"

Lyssa looked down at the plain gold band, then up into the eyes of the man she loved. "Oh, yes."